Ret

KT-232-583

Why the hell did it have to be Laurel who was the first woman he'd felt this kind of interest in since he'd come home?

The kind of interest that had his mind and body all stirred up. The kind of interest that made him want to take her to dinner, to wrap his arms around her, to touch her and kiss her and see where it led.

He squeezed the back of his suddenly tight neck and sighed. He had every intention of living the life of a model citizen and good father, putting behind him the wild reputation of his youth. The last thing he needed was an attraction to a woman who would be leaving soon, tempting him to enjoy a quickie affair that would grease the town gossip machine all over again. Gossip he didn't want his daughter to have to hear about her dad.

He'd keep his distance. But he couldn't deny that the thought of spending even a short time with interesting and beautiful Laurel Evans sounded pretty damned irresistible.

Dear Reader,

My family and I were lucky enough to spend two weeks in Greece this summer, and we had an amazing time—along with a few challenges that made the trip even more memorable! Like when our rental car broke down (twice) and the mechanic spent hours chatting to my husband and then sent a soda pop bottle filled with surprisingly good home-made wine back with him. :)

The people are charming and interesting—and of course the history is amazing and the entire country incredibly beautiful. I knew I wanted to set a book or two there, and since one of the many places I'd loved was Delphi I decided this one would take place there.

Andros, my hero, is a sexy Greek doctor who was training in the US until the shock of learning he had a small daughter sent him back to his hometown to raise her there. And, of course, archaeology had to be part of the story—so that's my heroine Laurel's passion! But she has a tragic reason for wanting to find the treasure her parents believed would be found there, and with only weeks left to make that happen she shouldn't let herself be distracted by a certain hunky doctor.

Except she *is* distracted! And avoiding spending time with him is impossible when several members of the archaeological team become seriously ill and Andros tries to figure out why.

This story is about both characters learning who they truly are and finally putting their pasts behind them so they can start a new beginning together. And there's an archaeological secret and a medical mystery thrown in for good measure!

I hope you enjoy Andros and Laurel's story. I'd love to hear any feedback you'd like to offer—you can write to me at Robin@RobinGianna.com or find me on my website or Facebook.

Thanks for reading!

Robin

HER GREEK DOCTOR'S PROPOSAL

BY
ROBIN GIANNA

First published in Great Britain 2015
by Mills & Boon, an imprint of Harlequin (UK) Limited,
Large Print edition 2015
Eton House, 18-24 Paradise Road,
Richmond, Surrey, TW9 1SR

© 2015 Robin Gianakopoulos

ISBN: 978-0-263-25519-5

Harlequin (UK) Limited's policy is to use papers that are natural, renewable and recyclable products and made from wood grown in sustainable forests. The logging and manufacturing processes conform to the legal environmental regulations of the country of origin.

Printed and bound in Great Britain
by CPI Antony Rowe, Chippenham, Wiltshire

After completing a degree in journalism, working in the advertising industry, then becoming a stay-at-home mum, **Robin Gianna** had what she calls her 'midlife awakening'. She decided she wanted to write the romance novels she'd loved since her teens, and embarked on that quest by joining RWA, Central Ohio Fiction Writers, and working hard at learning the craft.

She loves sharing the journey with her characters, helping them through obstacles and problems to find their own happily-ever-afters. When not writing, Robin likes to create in her kitchen, dig in the dirt, and enjoy life with her tolerant husband, three great kids, drooling bulldog and grouchy Siamese cat.

To learn more about her work visit her website: RobinGianna.com.

Books by Robin Gianna

Mills & Boon Medical Romance

It Happened in Paris…
Flirting with Dr Off-Limits
The Last Temptation of Dr Dalton
Changed by His Son's Smile

Visit the Author Profile page at millsandboon.co.uk for more titles.

A huge thank-you to my SWs:
Sheri, Susan, Natalie, Margaret and Mel.
You helped me through some tough times
with steadfast support and love. I appreciate
it, and all of you, so, so much!

A thank-you, as always, to Dr Meta Carroll,
for helping me with medical scenes
and always being there for me!

Thanks to my husband, George, for his
infectious disease expertise and endless
patience and support. Love you!

Praise for
Robin Gianna

'If you're looking for a story sweet but
exciting, characters loving but cautious,
if you're a fan of Mills & Boon Medical
Romances or looking for a story to try and
see if you like the medical genre, *Changed
by His Son's Smile* is the story for you!
I would never have guessed Robin is a
debut author: the story flowed brilliantly,
the dialogue was believable and I was
thoroughly engaged in the medical dramas.'
—*Contemporary Romance Reviews*

CHAPTER ONE

LAUREL EVANS GASPED as the pinhead-sized gleam of gold revealed itself, winking at her through the layers of dirt she'd painstakingly removed. Even mostly still buried in this pit they'd dug on Mount Parnassus, the glow was unmistakable.

Laurel's heart danced wildly in her chest as she grabbed her pick and brush, forcing herself to go slow as she gently worked to free the treasure. It took only a moment to realize it was something small, not the item she'd hoped to find, and she shoved down her brief disappointment. Oh so carefully, she used the delicate tools until the ancient find was finally loosened completely from the earth it had been long buried in.

A ring. Likely worn and possibly loved by someone thousands of years earlier. Even the smallest pieces of pottery, tools and partial bits of art they'd unearthed, reassembled and cataloged in the past weeks stepped up her pulse, but this?

Nothing beat the thrill of finding a treasure like this one.

No, scratch that. There was one thing she could think of that would be way beyond thrilling, and the weeks were ticking away on her hopes of finding it. Of getting it on the cover of archaeological magazines all over the world, along with her parents' faces, crowning the pages of her PhD dissertation, and ensuring funding for the next project that would get her own belated career launched at last.

She closed her fingers around the ring in her palm and breathed in the dusty, sweltering air. Too soon to panic. There were still a few weeks left before the end of this dig, and she, the rest of the crew and volunteers just needed to work harder and smarter. She looked up the mountain where the ruins of Delphi lay hidden from her view. Why couldn't the oracle still be there to advise her where the heck the mythical treasure might be deeply hidden on this mountain?

Laurel wanted to show Melanie what she'd found, but as she looked around at the crew working the numerous rectangular pits dug into the mountainside she didn't see her anywhere. Where could the woman be? Usually she was up early and on the mountain to enthusiastically guide her and the volunteers. Could she have gone to the caves with Tom? Seemed unlikely she wouldn't tell Laurel she'd be working with her husband instead of leading the mountain portion of the dig. Maybe the cold she'd been fighting had gotten worse, and she'd decided to sleep in.

Laurel swiped a trickle of sweat that persisted in rolling down her temple, despite the wide-brimmed canvas hat shielding her from the insistent sun. She tucked her exciting find into a sample bag, but before she could start to label it, her palm began to bleed again from under the bandage she'd put on it.

"Damn it," she muttered, trying to reposition the pad to cover it better, then ripped off a piece of duct tape to slap over the whole thing. So annoying that she'd stupidly jabbed herself while unearthing a sharp piece of what was likely part of a cup. She was just glad she hadn't further broken the artifact in the process. She started to label the ring bag again only to stop midword as her peripheral vision caught a movement nearby.

She glanced over to see a man walking up the

steep, rocky mountain path that wound between dried brown scrub scattered with tufts of thriving green plants, as steady and sure-footed as the goats that sometimes trotted by with their neck bells ringing. As he grew closer, she blinked, then stared. The brilliant sunshine gleamed on his short black hair and sent shadows and light across his chiseled cheekbones and jaw, his straight nose and sculptured lips. His face was so startlingly beautiful, so classically Greek, she thought he might be a mirage. That it was the god Apollo himself walking up Mount Parnassus to visit the temple built to honor him.

She gave her head a little shake, wondering if the blistering heat was getting to her. She narrowed her eyes against the sunlight and looked again.

Not her imagination. And not Apollo, but most definitely a real man. Greek gods didn't normally wear khaki-colored dress pants and a short-sleeved, blue, button-down shirt that was open at the collar. A shirt that emphasized the obvious fitness of his torso and the deep tan of his skin. A steel wristwatch caught and reflected the sun in little white diamonds that danced on the craggy ground with each measured step he took.

The one word that came to mind was *wowza*. Who in the world was he? And why was he wearing such a surprising choice of clothing for hiking the mountain in ninety-five degrees Fahrenheit? Must be a local businessman, or possibly a reporter come to check out the dig. Or, with his knockout looks, a movie star planning his next film. She didn't normally watch many movies, but if that was the case she'd definitely find time to fit in a viewing or ten of him on the big screen.

Laurel snapped out of her fixation on the man and finished her notation on the ring bag. She stood and quickly tucked the bag inside her canvas apron, next to her trowel. Tom and Melanie wouldn't be happy if she yakked to a reporter or anyone else before they even knew about her find.

He stopped to speak to one of the volunteers on the dig, who pointed at Laurel. The man's gaze turned to her, and even with twenty feet between them she could see his eyes were so dark they were nearly black, with a surprising intensity that seemed to stare right into her.

He resumed his trek toward her. He wasn't a

tall man—probably an inch or two shy of six feet. But the broad muscularity of his physique, which she'd noticed wasn't unusual among Greek men, made him seem larger. Or was it the sheer power of his good looks and intelligent gaze that made him seem that way?

"Are you Laurel Evans?" he asked with only a slight accent to his otherwise American-sounding words.

"Yes. Can I help you?"

"I'm Dr. Andros Drakoulias." He reached out to grasp her hand in a firm handshake. His palm felt wide and warm, slightly rough and not at all sweaty as she knew hers was. She pulled her hand loose and swiped it down the side of her shorts, hoping he hadn't noticed the sweat or that just the simple touch made her feel a little breathless. "Your colleagues, the two Drs. Wagner, asked me to let you know what was going on."

"Going on?" She realized it was a rather stupid echo of his words, but there was something about the serious expression she now saw in his eyes that sent her pulse into an alarmed acceleration. "Why? Is something wrong?"

"They came to the clinic early this morning

feeling feverish and ill. I've done some tests, and both have pneumonia."

"Pneumonia?" Laurel stared at him in shock. *Pneumonia?* How was that possible? "Melanie and Tom both had colds the past couple of days, but that seemed to be all it was."

"Unfortunately not. I have them on IV fluids and antibiotics, and I plan to keep them today and overnight at the clinic to see how they do."

Did this guy really know what he was talking about? Handsome didn't necessarily translate to smart. She studied him. Maybe it was wrong of her, but she couldn't help but wonder if the local town doctor had the knowledge and equipment to properly diagnose the problem. Should she take them to the closest large town instead, to be sure? "What makes you think it's pneumonia?"

A small smile touched his beautifully shaped lips. "Hippocrates could diagnose pneumonia by listening to a patient's chest, Ms. Evans. Ancient Greeks were at the forefront of medicine, after all. But believe it or not, even in our small-town clinic we have X-ray equipment and pulse oximetry to measure a patient's oxygen saturation."

Somehow, her face flushed hotter than it already

was beneath the scorching noon sun. "I'm sorry. I didn't mean to be insulting." Maybe inserting a little light humor into the awkward moment she'd created was in order. "But I must say, despite the Greeks putting the Omphalos stone at Delphi to show it was the center of the world, many believe Egyptian physicians adopted an ethical code of medical care centuries before Hippocrates."

His smile broadened; he was seemingly amused instead of offended, thank heavens. "Don't say that out loud, Ms. Evans, or you may find yourself in a no-win argument with angry locals."

"Is there any other kind of argument with Greeks?"

"Probably not." The amusement in his eyes became a dangerously appealing twinkle. "I lived in the United States for fifteen years. I know Americans think everyone outside the US and Western Europe are somewhat backward and simple. If you like, I could go up to the temple and consult Apollo. Or perhaps pray to Asclepios for guidance?"

"Not necessary. I'm sure you're very experienced, Dr. Drakoulias. I just…" Her voice trailed off, because she didn't know what else to say and had a feeling she might stick her foot in her mouth all over again. She sent him a grateful smile, hoping that would make him look past her blunder. "Thank you for walking all the way up here to let me know. Right now, I need to stay at the site to supervise since Mel's not going to be here. But I'd like to come down this evening to see them. Where's your clinic?"

"In Kastorini, which is at the base of the mountain above the gulf waters. Just follow the old bell tower to the center of town—you can't miss us."

"What's the address?"

His straight teeth showed in a smile that gleamed white against his brown skin. An unexpected dimple appeared in one cheek, which added another attractive layer to the man who sure didn't need it. "There are no addresses in Kastorini, Ms. Evans. We're small enough that everyone finds their way around without."

No addresses? How did people get their mail and things? She wasn't about to ask, though, and make even more of a fool of herself. "Well, I'm sure I can then, too. Thanks."

"I do have a question for you." All the teasing humor left his face. "Were both of the Drs. Wagner working in one spot? Somewhere they might have been exposed to a fungus of some kind?"

"Not really. Melanie is in charge of this part of the dig, and Tom leads the dig in the adjacent cave discovered a few years after the initial excavation. Why?"

"Just that it's unusual for two healthy people to come down with pneumonia at nearly the same time. Which makes looking for an external cause something we need to think about. Has Melanie been in the caves recently?"

Laurel thought hard about what they'd excavated and where they'd dug, but couldn't come up with anything that might have made them sick. "I'm almost certain she hasn't been in the caves at all. At least, not since the first days of the dig two months ago. At team meetings, Tom shares the cave dig results weekly, and Melanie shares our results. It's more efficient that way."

"All right. We'll see how they're both doing tomorrow and decide then if it makes sense to look harder for some connection." He looked around at the extensive excavation. "I wasn't living here when Peter Manago tried building a house in this spot and they found the ruins. When was that—five or six years ago?"

Had it been that long? Five years since her family's shocking loss that had turned her world upside down? A loss that seemed like yesterday, and yet, in other ways, felt like forever ago.

"I think that's about right." She swallowed hard at the intense ache that stung her throat. "Have you been up here to check it out?"

"No, but I've been wanting to. Is it filled with treasures offered to Apollo and the oracle?" His eyes crinkled at the corners. "Everyone who grew up around here used to dig giant holes—or at least giant to us—that we were sure would expose a sphinx, or the Charioteer's horses, or something else that would make us rich."

"And were you one of them?"

"Oh, yes. Born and raised in Kastorini. Many a goat has likely fallen into one of my 'digs.' But after finding only rocks and more rocks and the occasional very exciting animal bone, I decided becoming a doctor might be a better way to make money."

She had to laugh. Money was definitely not the

reason anyone dug in the dirt for a living. "No doubt about that."

"You must be finding something, though, or they wouldn't have been working at it for so long. What's here?" He looked around at the carefully plotted-out sections of earth. "Tell me about these squares you have marked off."

"Much of the time when you unearth a site that's several thousand years old, it's a bit like a layer cake. The oldest part of a settlement is at the bottom, with artifacts that reflect how the people lived then. Vessels used for cooking, style of art that's found, even the way a wall might be built, all can change a lot from the bottom of the cake to the top. But this site?" She loved sharing the excitement of this place with people who were interested. "The layers aren't there. There's no cemetery. No human remains, despite the number of buildings that housed probably a hundred people at a time. Which convinces us that it was temporary housing for pilgrims visiting Delphi."

"Interesting. How long, do you think?"

He stopped scanning the site to look at her with rapt attention in his beautiful eyes, and a dazzling smile that momentarily short-circuited her brain.

What had she been talking about, exactly? "How long what?"

"How many centuries did the pilgrims come to stay here?"

"Oh." The man probably thought she was dense. "About five hundred years, we think. Amazing that people came here to consult the oracle and worship Apollo all that time."

"Did the small earthquake we had a couple weeks ago damage anything?"

That earthquake had scared everyone, but especially Laurel. When the earth had rumbled around them, her heart had about stopped as the vision of how she'd been told her parents had died had surged to the forefront of her mind. The quake had lasted only a few minutes, but her insides had shaken for hours.

"Some rocks and earth loosened and fell into the pits, but it wasn't too bad, thankfully."

"That's good." He seemed to be studying her and she wondered what her expression was, quickly giving him a smile to banish whatever might be there. "Do you have any photos of the things you've found?"

"We do. A number of tools and potsherds have

been reassembled and I have pictures in a binder in that box. This section here," she said, showing him a large, cordoned-off rectangle, "is where several inscribed stones were found that are similar to the ones at the Temple of Apollo." And one of those stones was etched with the cryptic words that had convinced her mom and dad they'd find the priceless artifact Laurel was still looking for. That part had to be kept secret from most people, but she could show him the rest.

She pulled the reference binder from the supply box and flipped through it to show him a few of the best photos. They stood close together, the hair on his muscular forearm tickling her skin, his thick shoulder nudging hers, his head angled close enough to nearly skim his cheek against her temple. He smelled so wonderful, like aftershave and hunky man, that she found herself breathing him in. So enjoying his interested attention, she suddenly realized she'd gone on way too long.

"Sorry." She closed the book, feeling her face flush yet again, and not just from the blasting heat on the mountain. "I get a little overexcited sometimes."

"No. I'm fascinated." There was something

about his low tone and the way he was looking at her with a kind of glint in the dark depths of his eyes that had her wondering if he meant something other than the dig. That thought, along with how close he still stood to her, kicked her heart into a faster rhythm and made her short of breath, which she knew was absurd. But surely there wasn't a woman alive who wouldn't swoon at least a little over Andros Drakoulias.

"My sisters tell me that when I talk about my work, I need to remember to look for eyes glazing over when I go on and on. Sorry."

"Had you been looking, you'd have seen my eyes were most attentive. And you should never apologize for talking about something you love."

The deep rumble of his voice, the warmth in it, seemed to slip inside her, and for a long moment they just looked at one another, standing only inches apart, before Laurel managed to snap out of whatever trance he'd sent her into. She sucked in a mind-clearing breath and turned to shove the binder back into its box.

"You've hurt yourself." His strong arm came around her side, brushing against her as he reached for her hand. His head dipped close to hers again as he turned her palm upward, his fingers gently tugging loose the tape and bandage to expose the darn gash that had started bleeding again.

"It's nothing." She swiped at the trickle of blood, trying to tug her hand from his, but he held it tight. "I cut it on a potsherd. I'll bandage it up better when I'm done for the day."

"When was your last tetanus shot?"

"Just before I came here, Dr. Drakoulias. Cuts and scrapes are one of the hazards of this job."

"I know. Last summer, I had to treat one of the workers on this dig for sepsis." His gaze pinned hers, his former warmth replaced by a stern, no-nonsense look. "When you come to see the Wagners, I'll clean and bandage it for you."

She opened her mouth to assure him she could take care of it just fine, but the words died on her tongue. The wide palm that held hers was firm yet gentle, and something about his authoritative expression told her any protest would fall on deaf ears. Part of her didn't want to protest, anyway. She realized, ridiculously, that it felt…nice to have someone want to take care of it for her. Probably because, for a long time, she'd been the nurse, cook, decision maker and overall helper for her

sisters, without a soul to assist with all their challenges. Or, except for Tom and Mel, her own.

She reminded herself it wasn't as if there were
anything personal about it, the man was just doing
his job. "Not necessary. I have everything I need
to clean and bandage it at my hotel."

"Necessary." His eyes still on hers, he slowly
released her hand. "I'll see you at the clinic at,
say, six o'clock?"

It was loud and clear she'd be in for an argument if she refused, and what sane woman would
anyway? "Thank you. I'll be there."

The warmth of his palm lingered along with
a little flutter of her heart as she watched him
steadily stride back down the path, and she shook
her head at herself. Mooning after the man was ridiculous, supersexy or not, since the dig was over
in a matter of weeks and every second of her focus
had to be on what she'd come here to accomplish.

She was already so late getting her career
started. By the time her parents were her age,
their accomplishments had been featured in
numerous archaeological magazines. She could
still hear them pointing out how they'd finished
their PhDs in just four years, chiding their old-

est about her schoolwork and GPA, about how important it was to be a role model to her sisters. Doubtless they would be disappointed in her if they were still alive. She dropped to her knees to get digging again.

The best way, the only way, she could begin to catch up, keep their memory alive, and make them proud, was by doing whatever she could to finish their work then finally get going on her own.

CHAPTER TWO

HOURS LATER LAUREL was finally able to shower off the film of dirt that clung to every bit of exposed skin, before studying the cut on her hand. It was less than an inch long, but deeper than she'd realized, which was probably why it kept opening up and bleeding. She washed it out with peroxide and knew that it wouldn't be a bad idea to have Andros Drakoulias make sure it was clean. Which of course had nothing to do with liking the feel of her hand in his.

The feeble hair dryer in the old, rambling Delphi hotel that the excavation team had rented rooms in for the summer blew about as much air as she would trying to cool a bowl of soup. The impact on the dampness of her long blond hair was practically nil, and she had to wonder why she'd decided to dry it anyway, when she usually just pulled it back.

She shook her head as she wrapped an elastic

around her ponytail. Who was she kidding? She knew the reason, which was a certain megahunky Greek doctor her vain side wanted to look good for.

She threw on a sundress, swiped on a gloss of lipstick, and headed out of the door. Already perspiring again from the shimmering heat, she slipped inside the group's equally hot rented sedan. She nosed the car down the winding road out of Delphi, and, before she turned onto the highway, paused for a moment to take in the incredible view.

On every horizon, partly sheer cliffs scattered with pines met tumbles of boulders that looked as though they'd been broken apart then glued back together by some giant hand, or perhaps the gods and goddesses of Greek lore. The mountains cradled the valley below, filled with the distinctive silvery-gray leaves of an endless, undulating sea of olive trees that went on as far as she could see. Where the valley ended, the trees seemed to flow right into the Gulf of Corinth, the water such an incredible azure blue that, every time she saw it, she felt amazed all over again. And beyond that azure sea, another range of mountains met the sky that today was equally blue, but at times reflected an ethereal beauty when mistiness embraced the entire scene.

Just looking at it filled her with a reassuring sense of tranquility, the same way walking the ancient Delphi ruins did, hearing the voices of the past. Before she left, she'd take her camera on one last hike of this historic place that still felt so untamed. To remember it by.

With a last, lingering look, she turned onto the highway, her thoughts turning to Tom and Melanie. A bead of sweat slid down her spine as she wondered how they would be feeling when she saw them. Surely they'd have improved by now, since they'd been on antibiotics for hours.

For the first time all day, she let the niggle of worry she'd pushed aside grab hold and squeeze. After her parents had died, Mel and Tom had wrapped their arms around her as if she'd become their surrogate daughter. Advised her on grad school and now her PhD program. Helped set her up at digs close to home so she could still care for her sisters. Got her here as a paid assistant to work on her parents' project and her dissertation.

They were such special people. What if they were seriously ill?

No. Borrowing trouble was a sure way to have trouble take over, as her dad used to say. She'd had to be in charge at home whenever her parents were gone on digs, and full-time after they died. That had taught her a lot about leadership, and it was time to lead, not fret.

She had to get up to speed on what Tom's crew was supposed to be doing in the caves to make sure it happened. With so little time left on the dig schedule, not a single hour could be wasted by worrying. She knew Tom and Mel would agree, and that her parents would have too.

The sign for Kastorini was in both Greek and English, thank goodness. Laurel turned off the highway, concentrating on driving the steeply curving road that sported the occasional rock that had rolled down from the mountainside. And the term "hairpin curve"? Now she knew exactly what that meant.

If she hadn't already been sweating from the heat, this crazy trek would have done it. The road finally flattened and swooped toward a thick stone archway flanked by high, obviously ancient walls, and passing through it was like entering a different world. One minute she was driving with the mountain soaring on one side and dropping off on the other, the next she was surrounded by stone and stucco buildings sporting terracotta rooftops and draped with vines and magenta bougainvillea. Cheerful pots of flowers lined balconies and sat by inviting front doors. Farther down the narrow, cobbled street, men with small cups of coffee relaxed on patios in front of several tavernas, engaged in lively conversation as they watched her drive by.

The utter charm of the place made Laurel smile. And as Andros had promised, she easily spotted the ancient-looking clock tower and found the medical clinic with a few bona fide parking spaces right in front of it.

The building looked as old as the rest of Kastorini, and she wasn't sure what to expect when she went inside. A small, fairly modern-looking waiting room was currently empty, but within moments a young woman appeared.

"May I help you?" she asked.

The fact that, right away, the woman spoke English instead of Greek, proved Laurel's foreignness was more than obvious, though she'd accepted months ago that she didn't exactly blend in as a local.

"Hello. I'm Laurel Evans, working with the Wagners. I believe they're patients here? Dr. Drakoulias told me I could come see them."

"Ah, yes." Her pleasant smile faded to seriousness. "He is with a patient right now and wanted to talk to you before you see them. I am Christina, one of the nurses here. I will take you to Dr. Drakoulias's office."

Laurel followed the woman down the hallway. A side door opened, and she immediately recognized the deep rumble of Dr. Drakoulias's voice.

She couldn't follow many of his quickly spoken Greek words, but saw his hand was cupped beneath the elbow of a stooped-over elderly woman as they stepped from what looked like an examination room, obviously helping her stay steady as she walked. A small frown creased his brow just as it had when he'd been looking at Laurel's gash.

Whatever the woman said in return made him laugh, banishing the frown and making him look younger. His eyes twinkled as he shook his head, saying something else in a teasing tone, making her laugh in return. She lifted a gnarled hand to his cheek and gave it a pat, then a pinch that looked as if it had to hurt, but he didn't seem fazed.

Christina was chuckling too, as she took hold of the woman's other arm to walk with her back down the hall.

Laurel wanted to ask what the woman had said that was so amusing, and if she always pinched people like that, but didn't want to sound nosy. Dr. Drakoulias turned his attention to Laurel, and she felt the power of those eyes and that magnetic smile clear down to her toes. "Very punctual, I see. In my experience, the workers on the dig usually show up late. Or not at all."

"I admit it's easy to get distracted up there. But I had to learn fast how to keep track of time." Her own and everyone else's.

"So apparently you didn't find a gold statue today."

Her heart lurched hard in her chest and she stared at him, relaxing when she realized he was just kidding. "Not today, I'm afraid."

"Just so you know, I'd consider that a good reason to miss an appointment." He gave her a teasing smile that sent her attention to his beautiful mouth, which was not a good place for it to be. Thankfully, he reached for her hand and she followed his gaze to the new bandage. "Let's get this cleaned up."

"It's all right, really. I put peroxide on it and a clean bandage."

He grasped her elbow and walked to the sink, her injured hand still in his. "That's good, but I'd like to clean it again, nonetheless. Better to prevent an infection than have to treat one."

She couldn't argue with that, and again watched his fingers gently and carefully remove the bandage. He looked closely at her palm for a long moment before he spoke. "It's going to hurt a little, I'm sorry to say, but thoroughly washing this out is important. Are you ready?"

She nodded and braced herself as he turned on the faucet, holding the open cut directly underneath the cool stream. He was right, it definitely hurt, but no way was she going to be a baby about it. Biting her lip, she'd have sworn he about drained the town's entire water supply and was just about to yell, *Enough already!* when he finally turned it off.

He wrapped her hand with a towel and gently dried it. "You were very brave. I appreciate that you didn't scream in my ear like the last patient I did that to."

The eyes that met hers held a pleasing mix of humor, warmth and admiration in their dark depths. "I reserve screaming for activities that truly warrant it," she said. Then wanted to sink into the floor when his eyebrows lifted and something else mingled with the humor in his eyes. "Things like bungee-jumping, for example," she added hastily.

"I see. So you're a daredevil."

"Um, not really." Not about to admit she wouldn't bungee-jump unless her life depended on it, and definitely wouldn't admit the direction her thoughts had suddenly gone, she quickly changed the subject. "What is that stuff you're putting on there?"

"Just a topical antibiotic." With nowhere else to look, her gaze again got stuck on his face instead of his work on her hand. On his dark lashes, lowered over his eyes; his ridiculously sculpted cheekbones; his lips twisting a little as he wrapped white gauze over the cut. "This gauze bandage will keep it clean and dry, but I'd like to check it in a couple days."

"It'll be fine. Thank you." It suddenly struck her that she probably needed to pay him. "What do I owe you, Dr. Drakoulias?"

"First, I'd like you to call me Andros, since Dr. Drakoulias reminds me of my father and I don't want to feel old around a beautiful woman. Second, I'm the one who insisted on treating you, so it's on the house. I might get a bad reputation if I chase ambulances, then hand unsuspecting patients a bill."

She had to grin at the picture that conjured, and the smile in his eyes and on his lips grew in response. "So if anybody on the dig team gets hurt, I need to find a way to lure you to the site, then when your Hippocratic Oath kicks in, we'll get free medical care? Good to know."

"I'm pretty sure you'd have no trouble at all luring me there."

Did he mean, because he was interested in archaeology? Or something else altogether? After all, he'd called her "beautiful." She shoved aside the intriguing question, reminding herself she had work to focus on, and luring dreamy

Dr. Drakoulias couldn't be on the agenda, even if he was willing to be lured.

Though the thought alone put a hitch in her breath and sent a little electric zing from the top of her head to her toes.

"Are we going to see Mel and Tom now? Where are they?"

His expression instantly became neutral and professional. "They're in the clinic hospital, which is attached to this building. But before you see them, I'd like to talk to you in my office."

"Why?"

"Because," he said, his lips tightening into a grim line, "they are both seriously ill."

CHAPTER THREE

ANDROS WAS ALL too aware of the woman following close behind him down the clinic corridor. She smelled good. Like sweet lemons or grapefruit strewn with flowers, and he had an urge to bury his nose in the softness of her neck and breathe her in.

Something about her had stopped him in his tracks the first second he'd seen her on the mountain. Her blonde hair was the color of sunshine, pulled back into a thick, untidy ponytail that had flowed from beneath a creased canvas hat that was definitely for function, not style. The blue eyes that had met his were sharp and intelligent, and there was an exotic look to her features that made him want to keep looking. Maybe not a classic kind of beauty, but there was something intangible and appealing about her. Her skin was practically luminous without any makeup at all. He hadn't thought much about it until this moment, but, compared to the carefully put-together women he used to date, he liked her natural look a lot.

Down, boy, he reminded himself. Now wasn't the time to forget he was trying to reform the man who'd liked women far too much in the past, made-up, natural or anywhere in between.

Andros opened the door to his office and gestured for Laurel to go inside, wishing there were a little more room to move around. Usually he didn't notice how his father's old wooden desk that Christina joked was the size of an aircraft carrier practically filled the small space. At that moment, however, he was intensely aware of the close quarters.

Standing or sitting within inches of Laurel wasn't the best idea, since he kept finding himself distracted by her scent and her smooth skin and soft-looking hair. There wasn't much he could do about any of those problems, though, and he wanted privacy for this conversation. The last thing he needed was for a local to come into the clinic and overhear that there might be a contagion nearby.

"Have a seat."

She sat and turned to him as he lowered himself into the chair next to her, trying not to bump his knees into hers. He pondered for a moment, wondering how much detail he should give her about the Wagners' condition. She had to be worried, but instead of bombarding him with questions like a lot of people would, she waited patiently. He looked into her serious blue eyes and decided she could handle the truth, and deserved to know.

"Unfortunately, the Wagners are no better. I'm frankly surprised and concerned about that, after having them on IV fluids and antibiotics all day. As I mentioned before, I'm keeping them here overnight for observation. With any luck, they'll improve, but we should have seen some improvement already."

"Doesn't pneumonia usually respond to antibiotics pretty fast?"

"Often, yes, especially in younger people and those with no underlying physical problems, like the Wagners. That's the good news. But sometimes it doesn't. The truth about this situation, though? The presentation of their pneumonia is unusual."

"How so?"

"According to what they told me, Tom got what he thought was a cold a couple days before Melanie did. This morning Tom's respiratory rate was about thirty breaths per minute, Mel's twenty. Which indicates to me that she may have gotten it from him, which generally doesn't happen with pneumonia. Both are showing symptoms of the pneumonia worsening." He paused, hoping she wouldn't get upset at what he had to warn her about next. "If that continues into the morning, I will recommend they be transported to a fully equipped hospital in a bigger city about an hour away. It has twenty-four-hour skilled care and equipment we don't have."

Her lush lips parted in surprise. "You really think that might be necessary? Can't you just give them a different kind of antibiotic or something?"

"It's not that simple. I'm hopeful they'll improve and we can manage it here. I'm just making you aware that's a possibility. I'd prefer you didn't mention it to them, though. No need to worry them unnecessarily."

"All right." She nodded. "Are they...are they well enough for me to talk to them? If I have to take over leadership of the dig, I need to ask some questions. Find out more about the cave dig, since we were supposed to have our team meeting for the week tomorrow."

The eyes that met his were full of worry and alarm, and he wanted to reassure her but couldn't. He hadn't seen pneumonia with quite this presentation before and figured she might as well talk to the Wagners now in case the situation slid south—which he feared very well might happen.

He stood, and she did too, biting her full lower lip as she looked up at him. Standing so close he could have tipped his head down to kiss her. The instant that thought came to mind, he looked into her eyes, the idea now so appealing, so damned near irresistible, he had to inhale a deep breath and quickly step back. "I'll take you to see them now. They're on oxygen but will be able to talk to you. I want you to wear a surgical mask."

"You think I could make them sicker?"

"No. I think they might make you sick."

"Make *me* sick?"

Her eyes widened, and he wanted to make sure she understood the possible risk, because he damned well didn't want her to end up in the hospital too. "I told you before that it's unusual they've both developed this. We just can't know if it's possibly contagious or not."

He turned and led the way down the hall, again very aware of her walking closely behind as her sweet, citrusy scent wafted around him. He grabbed surgical masks from the supply cupboard outside the hospital wing and handed her one before putting on his own.

The Wagners were the only patients in the six-bed wing, and he was thankful for that. Tom Wagner lay motionless, his eyes still closed as they came to stand between the two beds, but Melanie Wagner opened her eyes and reached out to Laurel. She held Melanie's hand between both of hers, and Andros realized too late he should have had her put gloves on. Or at least one on her good hand, and warned her not to touch the Wagners otherwise.

He mentally thrashed himself. Until they knew what they were dealing with here, every precaution had to be taken anytime someone came in contact with them.

"I'm so sorry to have to dump all the work on you, Laurel," Melanie said in a whisper. "Isn't this crazy?"

"Don't worry about a thing, Mel," Laurel said, her voice slightly muffled through the mask. "I'll handle everything until you're feeling better. Dr. Drakoulias says he hopes the antibiotics will kick in soon."

"You won't have any problems leading the team until we're better. You've impressed me since day one on this dig." Melanie gave Laurel a glimmer of a smile. "Find anything good today?"

"Mostly more potsherds. But the most exciting thing was a gold ring. I'm pretty sure it's seventh century BC, but you'll know that better than I. Can't wait for you to look at it."

"Me either. I—"

A coughing fit interrupted her speech, and when she finally stopped, her breathing was obviously more labored. Laurel turned to Andros, her eyes wide.

He glanced at the quietly beeping screen next to the bed and saw that Melanie's respiratory rate had increased a little more from the last time he'd checked, which was not a good sign.

"Let's keep this visit brief, Laurel," he said, leaning close to speak in her ear. "The more they talk, the harder they have to breathe. Did you say you need to speak to Tom? I'll wake him and you can ask him a couple quick questions before you go."

He didn't want her to feel as if he was rushing her out, but didn't like the look of either of his patients. He adjusted the oxygen flow to both of them before rousing Tom with enough difficulty that it added another layer of worry.

"How are you feeling, Tom?"

The man opened his eyes and stared up at him, his mouth open, obviously having trouble breathing. "Hard to get air."

"I know. I just gave you a little more oxygen, which will help." Damn. Might not be waiting until tomorrow to send them to the Elias Sophia hospital, if they both continued to struggle like this. Andros turned to Laurel, but, before he had to say another word, she obviously got his unspoken message, since she quickly turned to Tom.

"I'm going now, so you two can rest and get better. Real quick, though, is there anything important I need to know about the cave dig that the volunteer crew can't tell me?"

"Just that we found some human bones. Exciting. Planned…" His chest heaved a few times before he continued. "Planned to share at the next meeting. I think they're older than the artifacts at the mountain site. Probably…Minoan, but…don't know…for sure yet."

"Okay. I'll talk to the crew and have them bring me up to speed. Don't worry about a thing." She patted his shoulder, and Andros stepped behind her to wrap his hands around her lower arms. She looked over her shoulder in surprise, but he couldn't risk her touching her eyes or pulling down her mask before she'd thoroughly washed her hands.

Her soft hair and enticing scent tickled his nose as he leaned forward to whisper in her ear. "I want you to wash your hands before you touch anything, especially any part of your body. Okay?"

She stared at him, then nodded slowly, saying a quick goodbye to both patients. Still holding on to the delicate wrist of her unbandaged hand, he led her across the room to the sink, squirted soap and stuck her hand under the faucet to wash it.

"I know how to wash my hands, you know."

"Except you're a bit handicapped right now. Can't wash the way you normally would, with one hand bandaged." As his fingers moved around and between hers, it struck him what an interesting contrast her hand was, like the woman herself. Slender, delicate, feminine fingers that were also hardworking and strong. "I want to make sure it's clean. The skin exposed on your other hand too, before I change the bandage."

"Change it? You just put it on."

"'Know Thyself' is one of the famous inscriptions at the temple." He kept washing, slowly now, enjoying too much the sensual feel of their hands soapily sliding together as he looked up at her, noticing the interesting flecks of green and gold in her questioning blue eyes. "My *yiayia* used to call me Kyrie Prosektikos, which means Mr. Careful. I believe in thinking things through and being appropriately cautious." Which had been true except for one notable aspect of his life he was determined to change. "So, yeah, I'm going to put on a new bandage."

"I'd say three bandages in an hour is careful, all right. If that doesn't sterilize it, nothing will."

He liked her smile. That she didn't roll her eyes or argue with him told him she trusted him, at least a little, to know what he was doing. "Glad to see you aren't doubting my doctoring skills anymore. Some of the tourists who come to this clinic never are convinced I know what I'm doing."

"What makes you think I'm convinced? Maybe I can just see you're hard-headed and bossy, and I don't have time to argue with you."

"Smart woman. You're right that I'd damned well get tough with you if I had to."

"Just remember I can get tough too. If I have to."

"Somehow, I don't doubt that for a second."

They stood there looking at one another, small smiles on their faces, before Andros realized he was just holding her hand in his, now, fingers entwined. He managed to refocus his attention on the job at hand instead of her captivating face and eyes, and very kissable lips.

Dried off and newly bandaged, Laurel paused as she was about to head out of the clinic door. "I'm worried, Andros."

He realized he liked the sound of his name on her tongue a lot better than the formal Dr. Drakoulias. When she looked up at him, her face filled with concern, he wished he could tell her she didn't need to be. But he was worried as well. "I know. I'm doing everything I can and will let you know how they are tomorrow. I'm planning to spend the night here to keep an eye on them. You have a cell-phone number I can call?"

"Reception is sketchy at the dig, but if you leave a message, I'll be able to get it when I'm back at the hotel." She scribbled her number on a piece of paper and pressed it into his palm, lingering there. "Promise to call me?"

"I promise." He folded his fingers over hers, squeezing gently to reassure her. It took effort to release her soft hand, to let her go. He stood there, motionless, to watch her walk to her car. Watch the gentle sway of her hips, the way her dress swung sensuously with each step of her drop-dead gorgeous legs. Watch the way her long silky ponytail caressed her back, until she'd gotten in her car and driven away.

He tucked the paper into his pocket and had a feeling he'd be tempted to call just to talk to her more about the dig. Just to hear her voice.

Which was foolish. The Wagners had told him the dig would be permanently over in just a few weeks and they'd be gone. She'd be gone.

Why did it have to be Laurel who was the first woman he'd felt this kind of interest in since he'd come home? The kind of interest that had his mind and body all stirred up. The kind of interest that made him want to take her to dinner, to wrap his arms around her, to touch her and kiss her and see where it led.

He squeezed the back of his suddenly tight neck and sighed. He had every intention of living the life of a model citizen—and a good father—putting behind him the wild reputation of his youth. Last thing he needed was attraction to a woman who would be leaving soon, tempting him to enjoy a quickie affair that would grease the town gossip machine all over again. Gossip he didn't want his daughter to have to hear about her dad.

He'd keep his distance. But he couldn't deny that the thought of spending even a short time with interesting and beautiful Laurel Evans sounded pretty irresistible.

"I know it's early, Dimitri." Andros paced up and down the hall of the clinic as he spoke to the infection specialist, barely noticing the dawn that rose over the mountain, filling the sky with pink and gold. "I wish I'd sent them last night. I wanted to give them time to possibly stabilize, but their respiratory rate's gone to thirty and forty breaths per minute. New chest films show dramatic worsening to progressive multilobar pneumonia."

"What's their oxygen saturation?" Dimitri asked.

"Both were hypoxic when they arrived. Now pulse ox says their sats have gone from ninety to eighty, even after giving them four liters of oxygen. This is acute respiratory failure, Di, and they may need intubation."

"Nikolaos will be here in an hour, and I'll send him right out."

Andros nearly slammed his hand to the wall. "We can't wait until the hospital's driver feels like rolling out of bed. Get him out here with portable oxygen now, or I'll bring them there. If they code on me, it'll be on your shoulders, since I don't have damned IV hookups in my car."

"All right, all right. He'll gripe like hell, but I'll have him there in an hour and fifteen."

"Good." He stopped his pacing to stare out of the window. "Get a blood test for fungal infection when they get there. I'm going to talk to the hotel management, and the archaeological crew they've worked with. See if I can figure out if there's some environmental cause."

"You think there might be?"

"Maybe. It's strange that they both fell ill days apart with the same symptoms. So make sure Nikolaos and the EMTs use infection control precautions, just in case."

"Will do. Talk to you after they get here."

Andros shoved his phone into his pocket, called Christina to come in early and keep a close eye on the Wagners, then caught up on paperwork in his office. He tried not to constantly check his watch. After forty-five minutes that felt like hours, he decided to make sure the Wagners were ready to go the second Nikolaos got there. He took a quick right out of his office, practically knocking down Laurel Evans, who was standing just outside his door. How had he missed her presence, when he'd been so acutely aware of it yesterday?

"Whoa, sorry!" he said, grabbing her arms to steady her. "Didn't see you there. Hope I didn't bruise you."

"No bruises. Though I did wonder for a second if I was on a football field instead of in a medical clinic." Her hands rested on his biceps as though they belonged there, and he had to stop himself from tugging her closer. "Now I see your real MO. Forget chasing ambulances. You injure people, fix them up, then bill them."

He smiled. "Not my MO. But I did play football in college in the US. Glad to know I still have the moves." Though knocking her down wasn't the move he'd like to make on her. "What are you doing here?"

"I couldn't sleep. So I came to see how they're doing."

The pale smudges beneath her eyes didn't detract one bit from her pretty face, and he again nearly pulled her against him instead of letting her go. To comfort and reassure her, of course.

"Not good." He gave her arms a gentle, bolstering squeeze before dropping his hands. "I've called the Elias Sophia hospital, which is about an hour away. The ambulance is coming to get them now."

"Oh, no!" Her hands flew to cover her heart. "They're worse?"

"I'm afraid so." He didn't feel it was necessary to tell her exactly how much worse they were. With any luck, they'd soon be fine and she'd never have to know the seriousness of the situation. "Sometime today, I'd like to talk to some of your people who've worked in the caves."

"To see if there's something there that made them sick." It was a statement, not a question.

"Yes."

"I'll be heading up when I leave here. The crew should be there soon, and I need to talk to them anyway. If you have time, you can come with me."

"Once the Wagners leave for the hospital, I can go. Even though Melanie hasn't been up there recently, it's worth asking a few questions."

"If it's contagious, just being in the same hotel room might have exposed her to it, right?"

"Right." He'd considered the same thing. The woman was smart, no doubt about that. "I'm also going to check with the hotel management, see if any tourists were ill, or if any staff that live elsewhere have been out sick."

"Can I see Mel and Tom now?"

"I'd prefer you didn't." Andros managed to temper the vehement *hell, no* he'd nearly responded with. But her being exposed to them again wouldn't accomplish anything. "Talking is difficult for them right now. After they're settled in at the hospital, we can go see them there together."

She tipped her head sideways and seemed to study him. Was she wondering if he had some ulterior motive in wanting them to go together? Again, smart woman. He hadn't said it for that reason, but as soon as the words were out of his mouth, the small rush of anticipation he felt spelled out loud and clear that, even if they were just driving to see his patients, and despite his concern for them, he'd more than enjoy the time with her.

"All right. But—"

"Dr. Drakoulias!" Christina came hurrying out of the doors of the hospital wing. "The hospital transport is here."

"Finally." He turned to Laurel. "Stay here. I'll be back shortly."

With Christina's help, he, the EMT and Nikolaos got both patients loaded in a matter of minutes. About to shut the ambulance doors, the scent of sweet citrus reached his nose. He looked over his shoulder, and saw Laurel standing right behind him, waving to the Wagners as they lay inside on their gurneys.

"Don't worry about a thing," she said, the smile on her face obviously strained. "I'll come see you with updates."

He shut the ambulance doors, yanked down his mask, and barely stopped himself from raising his voice at the woman next to him. "What part of 'stay here' and 'possibly contagious' are you not understanding?"

"I was a good six feet from them. It seems to me you're overreacting a little, since you don't know if they're contagious or not."

"There's a difference between overreaction and caution."

"Maybe that's just something you tell yourself." She folded her arms and stared him down. "Are you going to be bossy like this when we go up to the caves?"

"I'm only bossy when I have good reason to be." In spite of his frustration with her, he nearly smiled at the mulish expression on her face. She was toughness all wrapped up in softness. "So the answer is yes. I'm staying outside the caves and you are too."

"I'm an archaeologist, Dr. Drakoulias. Detective work is part of what we do. The Wagners are my bosses and my friends, and I'm going to do whatever I can to help. The caves are part of the excavation I'm doing my dissertation on, and, with Mel and Tom sick, I'm in charge now. I have to learn exactly what they're doing there and maybe in the process spot something that could have made them ill. Since I'm pretty sure you don't own Mount Parnassus, I'm going into the caves."

"You say I'm bossy? How about I say you're stubborn?" He let out an exasperated breath. "If there's a fungal contagion, possibly connected to the caves, no one should go in who hasn't been there already. Hell, no one should go in there, period, until we have some answers. But if they have to, they need to wear masks. Which I'll provide. You, though, have to stay out for now."

"Are you afraid Apollo's python may be lurking in there too, ready to strangle me?" Her voice was silky sweet, at odds with the sparking blue flash in her eyes. "Don't worry, I'll bring my bow and arrows just in case."

Clearly, the woman had serious issues with being told what to do. "Listen, Laurel, you—"

"Daddy!"

He swung around in horror when he heard his

daughter's little voice, and the sight of her standing just inside the door of the hospital wing with his sister and nephew, smiling her big bright smile, sent his heart pounding and adrenaline surging. His baby could not be in there when God knew what contagion might be in the very air. "Cassie. You can't be here right now."

"Why, Daddy?" Her eyes shone with excitement. "Is there really a python? I want to see!"

CHAPTER FOUR

LAUREL HAD BARELY blinked in shock at the little girl calling Andros "Daddy" when he'd strode to the child, snatched her up in his arms, hustled out the woman and little boy, too, and shoved the hospital doors closed behind them.

Heat surged into Laurel's face when she realized the man she'd been thinking of as dreamy Dr. Drakoulias, the man she'd been having some pretty exciting fantasies about all last night when she couldn't sleep, was apparently a married family man.

Why in the world had she just assumed he was single? Clearly, her instant attraction to him, along with wishful thinking, had blotted any other possibility from her mind.

Disgusted with herself, and, okay, disappointed too, she watched Andros crouch down next to the little girl. Surprisingly, he spoke to her in English. Why wouldn't the child speak Greek, instead?

"Cassie. There's no python. The pretty lady was just talking about the old story of god Apollo slaying the python dragon with arrows. Remember it?" The little girl nodded and Andros flicked her nose. "Know what, though? Remember when you didn't feel good with your tummy bug? There might be some germs in the clinic I don't want you to be around. I want you to go back with Petros and Thea Taryn, and I'll be home later."

Thea Taryn? Laurel didn't know a lot of Greek words, but she did know *thea* meant *aunt*. Which presumably meant the attractive, dark-haired woman was either Andros's sister or sister-in-law. Not that Laurel cared one way or the other, she thought with a twist of her lips. Married was married, and the thought of tromping over Mount Parnassus with him to talk to the crew together didn't seem nearly as appealing now.

Despite what she'd boldly stated, the truth was she didn't have a clue how to look for a fungus or whatever else could cause the kind of illness Mel and Tom had. She hadn't been in a lot of caves, but weren't most filled with all kinds of biological life she didn't know much about? Probably, she should simply focus on getting the excavation finished and hope no one else got sick. Getting it done was critical for a number of reasons, and Mel and Tom would doubtless want her to concentrate on that as well.

The cute little girl wrapped her arms around Andros's neck as he folded her close. Laurel's throat tightened as she watched the sweet moment, thinking of her own dad and all the times he'd held her exactly the same way. Thinking of how much he'd loved his four daughters, and how much they'd loved and admired him. Thinking how lucky the child was that Andros seemed to be a supportive and involved dad. One whose work enabled him to be with her all the time, and not away for months as her own parents had been.

She began to turn away at the same time Andros's head came up, and his eyes—dark and alive—met hers. He gestured to her to come over. She hesitated, then realized it was silly to feel embarrassed at her former hot fantasies. After all, he didn't know about them, thank heavens, and she was already over it. It wasn't as if she had time for any kind of relationship anyway, hot doc or not.

He stood. "Laurel Evans, this is my sister, Taryn Drakoulias, and her son, Petros."

That answered that question, she thought as they shook hands, though she should have seen the resemblance. Same dark hair, nearly black eyes and a slightly amused smile that implied maybe they both were privy to secrets no one else was privy to. His daughter had the same dark eyes, but her hair was a much lighter brown.

Laurel wondered if Taryn was divorced or had been a single mom, since she still used her maiden name. Or if she'd simply kept her name, but that seemed less likely, since Greece was still a very traditional country.

"This is my daughter, Cassandra." Andros smiled down at the girl, his eyes and face softened from the intense concern that had been on it just a moment ago. "Cassie, I'd like you to meet Laurel. She's an archaeologist, working on the dig up the mountain. You've learned a little about that, haven't you?"

"Yes! I have!" The child's eyes, so like her dad's, stared up at her. "Have you found lots of statues and gold treasures?"

If only. "Many things that are treasures to archaeologists, but not much gold, I'm afraid. Like father, like daughter, I see." Laurel smiled up at

Andros then turned back to Cassie. "Do you dig holes trying to find ancient treasure, Cassie, like your dad said he used to do?"

"Oh, no." She shook her head, her chin-length hair sliding across her cheeks as she did. "Fairies are scared of big holes. I don't want to scare them. I want them to sleep under our plants so they're in the shade and live in the little houses they build in the ground under special rocks. They stay cool that way."

"I see." Laurel's smile grew, remembering how much she'd loved pretend things as a little girl. Probably part of the reason she still loved classical myths today. "Have you seen the fairies?"

"Oh, yes." She nodded, very serious. "Sometimes they dance at night when there's a moon, and you can see them better. Sometimes they dance on my bed too, when they think I'm asleep."

Laurel looked at Andros again to see what he thought of his daughter's imagination. The lips she'd fantasized about were curved, and his eyes had attractively crinkled at the corners again.

No. Not attractively. Married, remember? Then again, he wasn't wearing a ring, so maybe he wasn't. That thought perked her up so much she nearly chuckled at how ridiculous she was being.

"We've made a fairy house out of stones, haven't we, Cassie? Have you seen any go in yet?" Taryn asked.

"No." Her little voice was filled with regret. "I think maybe I need to move the furniture around. Or put in something else. I don't think they like it the way it is."

Petros, who looked to be about five, chimed in, speaking Greek, but his mother stopped him with a hand on his shoulder. "English, please. It's good practice for you, and I don't think Ms. Evans speaks Greek." She turned to Laurel. "Do you?"

"Not much, I'm afraid. Trying, since I expect to spend a lot of time in various parts of the country on future digs, but it's not as easy as I'd hoped. I plan to study it more when the dig is over and I'm back at the university."

"Your work must be very interesting."

"It is. It also can be hot and dirty and takes a lot of patience, but the reward is worth it."

"Hot and dirty sounds like fun!" Petros exclaimed.

The adults' eyes all met, with Taryn looking

slightly embarrassed and Andros quite amused at the sexual connotation of what were, really, innocent words. Laurel should have felt a little embarrassed too, since she was the first to use the unfortunate phrase, but instead found the fantasies she'd enjoyed last night popped front and center into her mind. *Dang it.*

"What were you going to say about the fairy house?" Taryn hastily asked her son.

"I told Cassie we should make toad or snake houses instead. There's no fairies around here."

"Oh, there definitely are, Petros," Laurel said. "I'm sure there are plenty nearby." As soon as the words were out of her mouth, she regretted them. How ridiculous to defend Cassie's belief in fairies, when the child had her aunt and parents to pretend with her, and it was just cousin dynamics anyway, which made it none of her business. Must be habit from the fun she'd had making up stories for her little sisters. From defending them, too, she supposed.

"You know about fairies?" Cassie stared at her, wide-eyed.

"Ancient stories of fairies and nymphs and all kinds of things are part of what I do." The child was adorable, and she found herself wishing she could play fairies with her right then. But it was high time to change the subject and get back to work. "Speaking of which, I've got to get going. The students and volunteers are probably already at the sites by now."

"I'll go with you." Andros turned to his sister and spoke in a low tone. "The dig leaders are pretty sick, and I'm going to ask the workers some questions about where they've all been. For now, don't go into the hospital wing until it's been sterilized. I'll let you know when I'm done seeing patients this afternoon. I'll pick Cassie up then."

Taryn looked surprised, but nodded without comment before turning to Laurel. "Nice to meet you. Perhaps before the dig is over, you can come for dinner and tell us about all you've found in our backyard."

"Thank you, I appreciate the invitation." Having dinner with the happy Drakoulias family would be interesting, and she had to admit she was curious to meet Andros's wife. If he had one. So long as she could keep from drooling when she stared at the man the lucky woman was married to. "Nice for you to have all of Mount Parnassus as your backyard."

"Yes, Miss Laurel! And you can see our fairy house," Cassie said. "And help me get the fairies to come."

"I'd like that, Cassie." The child's bright eyes and smile would melt anyone's heart. It made her think of her sisters with a sudden longing to hug them. She was surprised at how much she missed them, considering she'd practically danced with joy when the youngest had started college this year and Laurel could finally get to this dig.

The dig. She glanced at her watch, dismayed to realize how much time she'd lost this morning. Time she couldn't afford to lose.

She turned to Andros. "Are you able to leave right now?"

He nodded. "Let me grab—"

"Dr. Drakoulias." Christina stuck her head out of the door. "We have a patient with a possible broken arm."

His lips twisted as his eyes met Laurel's. "Guess I'm not. How about I find you at the other site when I can, then we'll head over to the caves?"

"Okay." A mix of both relief and disappointment battled inside her as she said her goodbyes and headed to her car. She didn't particularly want him looking over her shoulder as she took over what would hopefully be temporary leadership and talked to all the dig workers. But she'd like to have him with her to ask the cave-dig volunteers questions she wouldn't know to ask.

And of course it had nothing to do with wishing she could just look at him and talk to him all day long…

The temperature thankfully dropped a few degrees when the sun sank behind the mountain. Laurel kept carefully digging and cataloging, ignoring the stinging ache in her palm, even though she'd let most of the crew leave long ago. Shoveling dirt and rocks and working in this kind of heat wore everyone down by the end of the day, and she couldn't expect them to be as intensely committed as she was. This dig hadn't been their parents' baby, and they didn't know about what Laurel still hoped was here somewhere, just waiting to be found.

Between her time at the clinic and meeting with different crew members, she'd lost more than half the day, and if she had to work until nearly dark to make it up, she would. So disappointing that Andros apparently hadn't been able to get away. She'd asked the volunteers at the cave dig to stick around later than usual, but, as far as she knew, he hadn't shown. Every time she'd seen someone move into her vision, her silly heart had kicked a little, until she'd realized it wasn't him after all.

Time to go to the cave site to tell everyone they were through for the day. Hopefully it didn't matter that Andros hadn't been able to talk with any of them. Maybe Mel and Tom would be better after their hospital stay, and they could all quit worrying about why they'd gotten sick in the first place.

She stood and stretched her tired back, shoved her things into her backpack, and turned to walk the half mile to the cave site, realizing too late how dusk was closing in fast. With her head down, she concentrated on staying on the goat path, well-worn through the scrub, her mind moving from Mel and Tom, to how she could possibly pick up the pace of the excavation without them, then to Andros and how unfair it was that a man she was attracted to more than any she could think of in recent memory was likely a married man.

"You make a habit of working until it's so dark you can barely see?"

Startled, Laurel nearly tripped over her feet, heart pounding as she looked up to see Andros's unmistakable broad form moving toward her on the goat path.

She pressed her sore hand to her chest, huffing out a breath of relief and annoyance. "You make a habit of sneaking up on people to give them a heart attack?"

"Well, we did talk about my MO being injuring people, fixing them up, then billing them."

"Uh-huh. Too bad for you my heart is still in one piece."

"Good to hear. And I wasn't sneaking." He stopped in front of her. "Just hoping to find you on the way to the caves, since you've kept your poor workers imprisoned there, saying they couldn't leave until you said so."

"I didn't keep them imprisoned," she said indignantly. "I was hoping you'd show up to talk to them, since you thought it was important."

"I'm sorry. We ended up having one injury or

illness after another, and I couldn't get away. Since they're still there, I'll go tell them they can leave now. I already spoke with two of them but wanted to find you before it got dark."

"I'll come with you." Being the team leader now meant she couldn't pass off her responsibilities to anyone else. Something she'd had to learn all over again every time she'd been frustrated, even a little resentful, at having to stay home to take care of her sisters. Her parents had made it clear that, as the oldest, that was her job, when all she'd wanted was to go along on their summer digs instead.

Finally, those responsibilities were behind her, and she was here on this amazing mountain. Except her parents would never be with her too. Her new responsibility was to their memory and what they'd always expected her to achieve with her life.

"I was going to insist you do, so I'm glad I don't have to." He smiled, his teeth shining white through the dusk. "Don't want you breaking an ankle walking down this mountain to your car in the dark. I parked not too far from the caves, so I'll drive you and the crew back to it."

"Are you saying I'm clumsy? Or do you always worry like this about everyone?" She smiled back at him, feeling the same silly little glow she'd felt when they'd been together here before and he'd wanted to take care of her hand.

"Clumsy? You're as graceful as a dancer, Laurel Evans. Kyrie Prosektikos is just being cautious."

The little glow grew warmer at the sincerity in his voice. "Because you don't want to fix another broken bone today."

"That too." He reached for her bandaged hand, rubbed his thumb across her knuckles. "How's it feeling?"

A little shiver snaked up her arm at his touch, and she nearly closed her fingers around his until she remembered she shouldn't. "Fine, thanks." She tried to tug away from his grasp, but he didn't let go. If she confessed that her cut actually hurt like blazes, he'd probably march her back to the clinic and torture her again.

"Good. Watch your step, and hang on to me." He tucked her hand into the crook of his elbow and, resting his wide palm gently on top of it, turned to head toward the caves.

They walked in an oddly companionable silence.

As she held his strong arm, the way he'd tugged her close to his body as they picked their way over the uneven ground felt oddly right. The intimacy of it, the evening sky beautiful with pinkly puffy clouds, filled her chest with a sense of calm pleasure, until she suddenly wondered if he knew she'd feel that way. If he was the kind of man who used his amazing good looks and charm to solicit affairs with women from the archaeological site, knowing they'd only be around for a while.

That unpleasant thought obliterated her sense of comfortable calm. "Tell me about your wife," she said.

It seemed there was a momentary hitch in his step, probably from guilt, and the chill that had filled her chest grew downright icy. "My wife?"

"Yes. Cassie's mother. Is she from Kastorini, too?"

"Cassie's mother was American. And we were never married."

This time, the hitch was in her own step. "Was?"

"Yes."

"I'm so sorry."

"Thank you, but she and I weren't…close. It's for Cassie you should feel sorry, since she barely remembers her. She passed away when Cassie was only two, and I got custody of her then."

He didn't offer more, and Laurel knew it would be rude to ask for details. The cold tightness in her chest turned to an ache for the little girl who would never know her mother. At the same time, it absurdly lightened a little at the thought that Andros Drakoulias was single and available. All the feelings of intimacy she'd felt just moments ago came surging back, making her hyperaware of how good it felt to be tucked against his warm, masculine body.

She mentally smacked herself. Maybe she couldn't shake this powerful attraction to him, but she wouldn't act on it. There was so much work to finish in so little time, and they were down two people to boot. Hadn't her mother always admonished her about never letting a boyfriend or crush get in the way of her focus on school or work? One hundred percent of her attention had to be on this dig and the important goal she still hoped to make happen.

Dusk had nearly given way to full darkness as they arrived at the entrance to the caves, and she released Andros's arm so no one would start any gossip, which at a dig could spread like poison ivy. Becka and Jason, two of the three volunteers, were packing up by the light of electric lanterns. "Where's John?" she asked.

"He's coming. Said he was working on unearthing another human bone and wanted to finish," Becka said.

"There's something I didn't ask before," Andros said. "Do each of you have your own section of the cave you work, or do you move around a lot?"

Becka swiped her hair from her eyes. "We keep to our own sections, mostly, unless Tom needs us to work somewhere else."

"Have you—?" Andros was interrupted by a violent coughing sound, echoing from inside the cave.

Oh, Lord, no. Laurel looked at Andros and saw his expression turn grim.

"Put these on. Now." He dug surgical masks from his pocket and quickly handed them out before putting one on himself. Another racking cough came from the cave just before John stumbled out, bending over and holding his chest for what seemed like minutes until it finally subsided, leaving him gasping.

Andros wrapped his arm around John's back, helping him stand upright. "You're burning up," Andros said, his voice slightly muffled through the mask. "How long have you been like this?"

"Had a cold the last couple days, like Tom. Got lots worse the past hour or so."

"Let's get you down to the clinic hospital and do some tests. My car's close by."

With John leaning heavily against him, Andros helped him down the path. Laurel's throat tightened when she saw Andros had taken a second to put on surgical gloves as well.

She hoped and prayed this was something completely different than what Mel and Tom were experiencing. That it was just a cold, and he'd be feeling better in the morning. Not horribly sick and hooked up to oxygen the way Mel and Tom had been. That Becka and Jason would stay healthy. That they'd all be fine.

But what if John got worse? What if his symptoms were exactly the same? And if they were, where would that leave the dig?

CHAPTER FIVE

"So what do you think?" Andros asked Dimitri in a low voice as they stood in the doorway of John Jackson's hospital room at the Elias Sophia Hospital. "Same thing as the Wagners?"

"Presents the same, but that doesn't necessarily mean it is. We'll have to wait for the blood tests to come back, and we won't have Mr. Jackson's until a few days after the Wagners'."

Andros looked at the woman standing next to the patient's bed and couldn't help but be impressed at how calm she seemed through all the activity around them. How steady, despite the incessant beep of monitors, nurses slipping in and out of the room, and techs checking the patient's vitals. Far calmer and steadier than he might have expected her to be, considering the heightened intensity in the air.

Though lines creased her brow and the blue eyes visible over the surgical mask she wore held a deep concern, her composure didn't waver. She stood straight, talking to John about the dig.

Andros had already transferred the patient here this morning, just before Laurel had shown up at the clinic. When she'd asked for directions to drive here after the day's work at the dig, he'd instantly offered to bring her instead, wanting to see the Wagners and John, too. And if an hour's car ride enjoying her scent in his nose and conversation from her lush lips was part of his motivation, what was the harm in that?

When he'd first introduced her to Dimitri, she'd asked good questions, her responses intelligent and thoughtful. She hadn't overreacted or panicked, simply displaying clear leadership in taking over for the Wagners.

Andros's heart knocked in his chest when he saw her reach out to touch John's arm, relieved when he saw her hesitate and withdraw it. John said something Andros couldn't catch, and a smile touched her eyes as she answered him back then said goodbye. She turned toward the door, and her eyes met his, held.

"You have something going with the pretty lady?" Dimitri asked.

The surprising question had him breaking eye contact with Laurel to stare at his friend. "I just met her two days ago."

"Sometimes only takes two minutes."

And damned if that wasn't the truth. Or even two seconds, which was about how long it had taken for his interest to go from zero to sixty the first moment he'd laid eyes on her.

"And if you don't, you should," Di said in a lower voice, grinning and waggling his thick eyebrows like Groucho Marx. "I'll keep you posted on our patients." He headed down the hall as Laurel joined Andros at the doorway.

"John seems to be holding his own. Doesn't he?" Her questioning eyes seemed to be willing him to reassure her. "He doesn't seem to have as much trouble breathing as Mel and Tom did when I first saw them in your clinic hospital."

"Not at the moment. Hopefully he'll stay that way." He wrapped his fingers around her arm and drew her farther into the hall. "Di told you we just don't know if this is the same thing the Wagners have or not. An influenza or some other virus. Bacterial infection or fungal infection."

"When will you know?"

"Di asked to have John's test results expedited, but that will still take a couple days."

She nodded, that pucker of worry still on her face. "I'm so relieved, though, that Mel and Tom aren't any worse. Do you think they'll be released soon?"

"Hard to say. They're getting good care, so we'll keep our fingers crossed." He wanted to banish, for at least a little while, that deep concern clouding her eyes. There was nothing more to do here, and a glance at his watch showed it was already well past 7:00 p.m. "How about we have dinner here before we head back?" He'd thought of that, wanted that, from the moment they'd left Delphi to drive here. Time spent with her away from her work and his, away from Kastorini, away from the serious problems on both their minds.

"I probably should get back. Update the team and make sure they're okay."

"Why wouldn't they be okay?"

"Well, they…" Her voice trailed off and she gave a little rueful smile. "You're right, they're adults. I forget sometimes I don't have to play mom anymore."

"When did you have to?" Surely she didn't have

children. Leaving them for the entire summer for the dig.

"Oh, for my sisters. It's a wonder my hair's not prematurely gray." The tone of her voice had lightened and she smiled. "The dig team has explored a few towns outside of Delphi on weekends, but not here. So dinner sounds lovely."

"Good." He let go of her arm, resisting the urge to hold her hand instead, and they headed to his car. "You in the mood for seafood, or Greek food, or both?"

"Anything. Everything. I didn't have much lunch, and I have to admit that, next to digging, eating's one of my favorite things to do."

"Yeah?" She'd obviously decided to let herself relax with him, to let go of her worries for a time, and he grinned at the sudden enthusiasm in her voice. "Something we have in common. I know just the place you'll like."

It was only about a ten-minute drive from the hospital to the waterfront, and, since it was early yet for locals to be eating dinner, he had no trouble finding a parking spot. "Sit tight," he said to Laurel as he got out of the car, going around to her side of the car to open her door.

"More of your worrying I'm clumsy?" she asked as he held out his hand to her. "Getting out of a car isn't quite as dangerous as walking down a rocky mountain in the dark."

"Being a gentleman pleases me. And because I can see you're a woman who cares about others, you won't mind indulging me, will you?"

"Ah, the charm of Greek men." She shook her head, but a smile tugged at the corners of her lips.

She placed her soft hand in his and stepped from the car. It felt so nice to hold it, just as it had when he'd washed her palm at the clinic, and he couldn't seem to make himself let go. A little surprised that she didn't release his either, he gave in to enjoying the simple connection. Stars began to wink in the darkening sky as they strolled down the brick promenade that went for a good quarter mile along the lapping gulf waters.

"I've been in Greece two months, and I'm still amazed at all the little restaurants that line the water in every town," she said, gazing at the lanterns and lights beneath huge umbrellas connected together, one after another. "So pretty. With comfy seats too, if you want, instead of a table. I wish there were more places like this in the States."

"I went to med school in New Jersey," he said. "I admit I never got used to the beach restaurants there. Always wanting you to move on your way right after you're done. In Greece, you're expected to eat and relax for the night."

"Somehow when you said you lived in the US, I was picturing LA or Montana."

Her eyes were filled with a teasing look, and he found himself drifting closer until his shoulder brushed hers. "LA or Montana? First, I'd say those two places don't have much in common, and second, I'd ask why."

"I'm not sure." She tilted her head at him, seeming to size him up, and he grew even more curious about what she was thinking. "Maybe because you seem sophisticated and at the same time rugged. Like a Greek cowboy."

Sophisticated but rugged sounded pretty good. As if she might find him attractive, and he certainly found her very attractive. "I'm more of a Greek goat boy than a cowboy, since it was my job to look after ours when I was a kid."

"Goat boy?" She laughed. "Sorry. Doesn't work at all for you."

"You might change your mind if I show up smelling like one of Cassie's goats sometime. She and Petros like to pretend they're horses and bring them into the 'stable.' Which is her name for our living room."

"Oh, my gosh, that's adorable."

"Not when your house smells like a barn."

Her laugh, the sparkle in her eyes, were sheer temptation. The kind of temptation that left Andros wondering if he could possibly resist. If he could keep his hands and lips to himself when all he wanted at that moment was to pull her close and kiss that smiling mouth.

He drew in a deep breath, glad they'd arrived at one of his favorite restaurants, interrupting his dangerous thoughts. "Would you like to sit at a table, or have *mezedes* on these seats looking out over the water?"

"*Mezedes?*"

"You've been in Greece two months and don't know what *mezedes* are?" He teased her with mock astonishment. "Appetizer-sized plates for dinner, instead of one entrée. Eating various *meze* over a whole evening, preferably with ouzo to drink, is a Greek tradition."

"Ouzo? You're kidding. That stuff is awful!" He had to grin at the cute way she scrunched up her face. "Mel and Tom had us all try it at dinner in Delphi one night and I could barely swallow it."

"Don't worry. Ouzo's optional."

"Good, because the *meze* sounds wonderful. I like trying different things. And I want to enjoy seeing the water while I still can."

A reminder that she wouldn't be here for long. But when it came right down to it, what did it matter? He wasn't capable of futures or happy-ever-afters with a woman anyway. And they were far enough away that he didn't have to worry about the gossip Kastorini townsfolk used to love to share about him, back in the careless days of his youth. Which had extended into too many care-less days with women in his adulthood, too.

They sat side by side in the cushioned wicker seat, and it took effort to concentrate on the menu instead of how close she was, how good she smelled, how pretty she looked. "So, no ouzo," he said. "What do you like to drink?"

"White wine, but don't let me stop you from drinking ouzo."

No way he'd be drinking ouzo. If he kissed her, he wasn't about to taste like the licorice liquor she hated. Then reminded himself that kissing wouldn't be a good idea. "Have you ever tried retsina?"

"No. That's a Greek wine, isn't it?"

"Another thing that can be an acquired taste. Some people think it tastes like turpentine, or pinesap, but by the third glass, you'd like it."

"Third glass? Are you trying to get me drunk to take advantage of me?" He hadn't seen this mischievousness in her eyes before, and his heart beat a little faster as he thought of ways they could take advantage of one another and how much fun that would be. "How about I stick with sauvignon blanc?"

"I'm a gentleman, remember?" A gentleman who wanted to kiss her, wanted to know whether this attraction, this awareness, went both ways. Except he shouldn't want to know, because if she felt any of what he was feeling he'd find it even harder to keep their relationship strictly friendly and uncomplicated. "We'll get both, since you like to try new things."

"Far be it from me to not try a drink that tastes like pinesap."

Even as he grinned he wondered how her mouth would taste no matter what she'd been drinking, and yanked his gaze from her lips, handing her the menu. "What sounds good?"

She handed it back. "You've heard the phrase, 'it's all Greek to me'? Unfortunately, studying ancient languages doesn't help me read one word of that."

"Sorry. How about I order a few of my favorites, then we'll go from there? Grilled octopus, *keftedes*, which are fried meatballs I personally could eat a dozen of, peppers stuffed with feta, and olives from the valleys by Kastorini to start."

"Sounds wonderful, except maybe the octopus. Can't wrap my brain around eating those little suction cups."

She gave an exaggerated shudder that was almost as cute as her ouzo expression. "Maybe you haven't had them cooked properly. And I'm beginning to learn you're a little overdramatic at times, perhaps."

"Perhaps." Her lips curved. "I love that the olives are from that sea of trees. It's incredible how many there are."

"Over a million. And many are over a hundred years old."

"A hundred? That's a nanosecond in Greece."

"Says the archaeologist, not arborist."

They smiled at one another until the waiter showed up to take their order, then brought the wine. Andros let himself enjoy looking at her over his glass. Wished he could see her with that long, thick, silky hair of hers out of its restraint and spilling down her back. He nearly reached to grasp the ponytail in his palm, wanting to stroke the length of its softness with his hand, but stopped himself.

"Tell me about being mom to your sisters. How many do you have?" he asked, as much to keep from thinking about touching her as genuinely wanting to know more about her. Then instantly regretted the question, surprised to see the beautiful eyes that had been relaxed and smiling become instantly shadowed.

"Three younger. One just graduated college, one's a sophomore, and the youngest, Helen, is on a summer internship in Peru before she starts as a freshman in a few more weeks." She stayed quiet for a moment, and Andros was trying to figure out if he should start a different subject when she finally spoke. "My parents were the archaeologists who started this dig and were killed that first summer. That's how I came to take over the mom role. Did a pretty bad job of it half the time, but I tried."

"I'm so sorry. What happened?" His heart kicked at what a shocking loss that had to be. He put down his glass and rested his hand between her shoulder blades. "You must have barely been, what, twenty-two?"

She nodded. "I'd graduated college that May, and just a couple weeks later they came here to start working the dig. I was home watching my sisters. My parents were excavating a new pit and were inside it deciding how much deeper they could use machinery, when an earthquake hit. The rock walls collapsed on them."

"Dear God. I remember that earthquake's epicenter was right here on Mount Parnassus, and that some of the buildings in Delphi and Kastorini were pretty badly damaged. I can't believe your parents…" He trailed off, unable to imagine it. The shock of such a freak thing taking both of her parents at once.

"I know. It was…unbelievable. Devastating for us girls."

"That small earthquake a couple weeks ago must have scared the hell out of you. Brought it all back." She nodded, and Andros's chest squeezed at the pain on her face. "So you took over for your parents, taking care of your sisters."

"The court allowed me to become guardian. I'd watched them every summer anyway, when our parents were gone on digs. We managed. Survived. I'd planned to start grad school, but had to put it off for a few years. I hate that I'm so behind what my parents groomed me to accomplish by now. Far behind all that they'd accomplished by my age, but there wasn't another good option. It's…I knew it was what they would have expected, even though they would've been disappointed that school had to come second." The tears came then, squeezing his chest even tighter, and she quickly dabbed them before they could fall. "Sorry. Stupid to cry after all this time."

He couldn't figure out how much of her tears

were from grief over her parents, or the pain of believing, somehow, that they would be disappointed with her. Surely she didn't really feel that way, considering how she'd stepped up and put her sisters first. At twenty-two, he'd been damned self-absorbed, for sure.

He took her chin in his fingers, turned her face so she was looking at him. "Never be sorry for being human and feeling pain, Laurel. Grief stays with us, sometimes for a long time. Until we learn what we have to from it to move on."

The way she forced a smile through her tears gripped his heart, and without thinking he lowered his head an inch and touched his lips to hers. Softly, gently, meaning to soothe. They were soft and pliant beneath his, and for a long moment the kiss was painfully, wonderfully, deliciously sweet.

They slowly pulled apart, separating just a few inches, staring at one another. Heat and desire rushed through his veins like a freight train just from his lips on hers. A heat and desire that had him wanting to go back for more, deeper and hotter. He fiercely reminded himself she was hurting, that he was supposed to be offering comfort. Not consumed with the need to lay her down on the cushioned seat and kiss her breathless.

Her eyes were wide, and inside that deep blue he thought he saw a flicker of what might be the same awareness, the same desire. Just as he began to ease away from her, she surprised the hell out of him, wrapping her palm behind his head, closing the gap between them and kissing him back. He found himself grasping her ponytail as he'd wanted to earlier, gently tugging her hair to tip her face to the perfect angle, letting him delve deeper. Her lips parted, drew him in as he learned the dizzying taste of Laurel Evans.

"Ahem. Your peppers and *keftedes.*"

They both slowly broke apart, and Andros struggled to remember they were in a public restaurant before he turned to the waiter. "Thanks."

The waiter responded with a grin and a little wink at Andros before he moved on to another seat farther down the promenade. He looked at Laurel, not surprised to see her cheeks were a deep pink. Hell, he had a feeling his might be too, and didn't know what to say. Maybe something along the lines of, *Sorry, I didn't mean to try to suck your tongue like you were the first* meze, *but you taste so good I couldn't help myself.*

He cleared his throat. "I—"

"You were wrong, you know," she interrupted in a soft voice.

"Wrong?"

"That I'd need three glasses of retsina before I'd think it tasted good. Just one taste from your mouth, and I know it's very, very delicious."

That surprised a short laugh out of him. "And I've come to have a new appreciation for the very appetizing flavor of sauvignon blanc." Her words, her smile, the heat in her eyes that reflected his own, nearly sent him back for another taste of her, but he somehow managed to keep his mouth to himself. He slid the plates of food closer to her. "Try the *keftedes* alone, and then with the *tziaziki.* Which, by the way, we either both have to eat, or neither of us."

"Why?"

"Because I don't want to smell like garlic if you don't. But if we both do? Nothing like a garlicky *tziaziki* kiss, I promise." And why had he brought up the subject of kissing when he was trying to behave?

He was glad to see every trace of sadness was gone, replaced by a slightly wicked smile that sent his blood pumping all over again. "Don't think it could beat the last one, but I'm more than willing to give it a try."

"I doubt it could beat the last one either. Guess we'll have to find out."

The memory of that kiss had the air practically humming as they looked at one another, and Andros knew he had to bring the conversation back to something less exciting to ratchet down his libido. Either that, or leave and steam up the windows of his car.

And that idea was so appealing, he nearly threw money on the table and grabbed her hand to get going on it.

"So," he said, stuffing half a meatball into his mouth to drown out the flavor of Laurel, "I assume you're going to shut down the cave dig for the moment."

"Shut it down?"

"Yes. With John sick now too, it's logical until we get some test results back."

"We only have a few weeks left of the dig as it is. And no one has any idea if they're sick because of something in the caves or not. For all we know it could be something a tourist brought to the hotel. Or even coincidence and not the same illness."

He was surprised as hell at her attitude and the suddenly mulish expression on her face, especially considering she'd seen how sick the three were and had seemed as worried as he was. "True. But it makes sense to wait until we get the test results. How could a few days matter?"

"Every hour matters. There'll be no more funding for this project. Which means whatever we have left to unearth has to be discovered soon, or it'll stay buried."

"Things will stay buried anyway. Unless a dig lasts indefinitely, I'd think you could never be sure what might still be there."

"True. And we have used satellite imaging and ground-penetrating radar and magnetometry to help us find what's still there. But those things are less reliable when it comes to the caves."

"So you're willing to risk someone else getting sick to give yourself a few extra days' digging." He couldn't help but feel frustrated, even angry about that, especially when an image of Laurel lying in a hospital bed, sick and nearly unable to breathe, disturbingly injected itself into his mind.

"I need to finish this dig for my parents." She frowned at him for a long moment before she finally spoke again. "But I'll compromise. I'll offer the team a choice about working on the mountain, and we'll stay out of the caves until the test results are back. Unless you can prove to me the pneumonia is definitely related to the dig, though, I'm not shutting it down."

CHAPTER SIX

"I CAN'T BELIEVE Kristin stayed at the hotel when we're already down three people." Becka sat back on her haunches and pushed her hair under her hat as she looked over at Laurel.

"It's fine, Becka." Laurel pulled a bag and pen from her apron to label the potsherd she'd dug up. "The reason I shared Dr. Drakoulias's concerns with the team was to give everyone the option to sit it out until the test results are back, if that's what they're most comfortable doing."

"But how could it have anything to do with the dig? We've been here two months with nobody getting sick."

"I agree. But until we have confirmation that it's not a fungal infection, I think everybody has the right to be extra cautious if they want, and we'll stay out of the caves for now."

"I don't get why he thinks there might be something in the caves. Mel hasn't been in there since June."

"It's possible she got something from Tom. But I figure it's more likely they got some random virus from some long-gone tourist while we had dinner in Delphi, or someone who stayed at the hotel. Though Dr. Drakoulias and I have both talked to management there, and as far as they know, nobody's been sick."

"So we should just keep at it, don't you think?"

"I'm planning to, but, again, I understand people being concerned. We all want this dig to end on a high note. Hopefully the three of them will be fine soon, and we'll find there's nothing to worry about." She prayed that was true, and that the high note was a certain big, knockout find she hadn't given up on.

"Well, I'm not worried about it. And I've gotta say, I'd rather be in the nice, cool cave than out here all day. I'd forgotten how beastly hot it is."

"Working in heat, cold and rain is part of the gig sometimes. And don't forget about the snakes up here. Gotta be tough to be a digger." Laurel smiled and tossed a water bottle to Becka. "We'll quit for the day in about an hour. Hydrate and take a little break."

Becka stood and swigged down some water. Laurel's smile grew at how much the girl reminded her of her sister Ariadne, and as she was wondering what her siblings were doing, Becka interrupted her thoughts with a chilling scream. Her heart knocked against her chest when Becka dropped the bottle and fell, writhing, onto the ground.

"What's wrong?" Laurel leaped to her feet and ran the few feet between them.

"Oh, God, my leg! What...?"

Laurel followed the girl's wide-eyed gaze, horrified to see that beneath the hand clutching at her calf, blood gushed down her leg, a shocking amount pooling around the dirt and stones she lay sprawled on.

"Becka. Let me see." Laurel's heart pounding now, she dropped to her knees and instantly saw what had happened. "I think your trowel cut you."

"I'm so stupid," the girl moaned. "You always said never to stick our trowel in our back pocket, but I did, didn't I? Did it cut through my shorts and fall out? Is it bad?"

"It's a pretty good gash." That was an understatement, but the last thing Laurel needed was for the girl to faint or go into shock. "Let me get it wrapped up, then we'll have to get you down the mountain somehow."

Her mind frantically spun to first-aid classes she'd learned, and she prayed she remembered right. The injuries her sisters occasionally came home with had been pretty minor. Definitely nothing like this. Laurel had seen a few injuries on the digs she'd been able to go on close to home but hadn't been in charge. Why hadn't she paid more attention to how they'd stopped the bleeding?

Okay, she reminded herself grimly, freaking out and staring at it wasn't going to fix it. She ran to the supply box and dug through until she found gauze wraps on the bottom and the duct tape she'd used over her bandage. But when she kneeled next to Becka, the amount of blood pouring through the girl's fingers sent fear surging down her spine, and she knew she had to do something more than just wrap it.

"I'm going to try to hold it together and put pressure on it for a few minutes to slow the bleeding before I wrap it. Okay?"

Becka nodded. Just as Laurel began to lay a piece of gauze lengthwise on the cut, the girl let out a little moan, and Laurel looked up at her. Lord, she was staring at the blood, her face turning the ghastliest white. "Don't faint on me now." That was the last thing either of them needed, and Laurel quickly tried to move her into a sitting position.

"Sit up and put your head between your knees." It wasn't easy to press on the wound at the same time she pushed the girl's head down with the other. "Deep breaths. I'm going to press hard on your leg to stop the bleeding, so be prepared."

Becka thankfully followed directions. Every muscle tense, Laurel tried to gently bring the edges of the wound together, then pressed hard again. Becka cried out, biting her lip until Laurel was afraid it might start bleeding too. "I'm sorry. Hang in there. Once I get it wrapped up, I'll take you to Dr. Drakoulias."

As soon as the words were out of her mouth, her heart knocked again. What if the man wasn't in Kastorini, but back at the Sophia Elias hospital or somewhere else? Then she remembered she had his phone number. She'd call him as soon as she could get a cell signal.

The fear filling her chest eased a bit, and she took a deep breath. It would be okay. No matter where he was, she'd be able to ask for his help. How much that thought calmed her was a little shocking, considering she hadn't relied on anyone else for much help in a long time.

She just hoped he wasn't still annoyed with her the way he'd been last night. Then wondered why she'd let it bother her. Her job, her responsibility to her parents and the future they'd wanted for her were all wrapped up in this dig, and she couldn't care if anyone approved of how they finished things up or not.

"Can you press down on it the way I was while I wrap it? Try not to move the gauze I already have on there."

"Okay," Becka said in a strained voice, reaching down to do as Laurel asked. Finally she had it tightly wrapped, hoping to heck it wasn't so tight that it cut off the poor girl's circulation. She sat back on her heels and stared at the gauze, relieved that it wasn't turning red with more blood.

"Okay, let's go. I'll help you stand, then we'll grab Jason so he can help us."

With Becka's arm across Laurel's shoulders, they awkwardly moved down the path toward grid eight. She couldn't see Jason, and prayed he was down in the pit where he should be. By the time they got to it, Laurel already felt nerves and muscles pinching from trying to hold Becka's weight as she limped. "Jason! Are you here?"

"I'm here," a voice said.

Laurel nearly sagged in relief. "Becka's hurt. I need your help."

In an instant, Jason came running up the makeshift stone steps from the pit, a worried frown on his face. "What happened?"

"I stupidly put my trowel in my shorts pocket, and it cut through and dove into my leg," Becka said through clenched teeth.

"Rookie mistake." Jason gave Becka a little smile as he lifted his hand and stroked her cheek, the gesture tugging at Laurel's heart. She'd thought maybe the two college kids were becoming sweet on one another, but hadn't paid that much attention. "You okay?"

"I think so. Hurts like crazy, though, and I'll probably have some ugly scar."

"Scars from a dig are a badge of honor. Makes you all the more interesting."

"You think?" The girl rolled her eyes at him, finally looking less freaked out.

"Oh, yeah. Not that you needed to be more interesting."

"Okay, enough of the mushy stuff, you two," Laurel joked, glad to be feeling less freaked out too, after the first shock of it all. "Let's get her down the mountain to my car so I can take her to the clinic. It's pretty deep, and I'm sure she'll need stitches."

It was easier with Jason's help, or, really, with Laurel helping Jason, who took on most of Becka's weight. Laurel called Andros a few times, relieved when she finally got a signal and he answered.

"Is something wrong, Laurel?"

How had he known it was her? The man must have put her contact information in his phone. That thought shouldn't have affected her, since he probably did it for professional reasons, but she couldn't help feeling absurdly pleased about it. "Becka has a serious gash in her leg from a trowel. Are you at the clinic?"

"I'm here. Bring her right in."

Jason got Becka tucked into the car and hovered there as he fastened her seat belt. "I'd like to come with you, but I better get back to work. At this rate, we're not going to finish what we've started if I don't."

"I'll be coming back to the dig after we get her fixed up and settled in at the hotel. I'll let you know how she is," Laurel promised, partly to relieve his mind and partly to get going before there was some long, drawn-out goodbye. Becka's leg needed prompt attention. And he was right— they'd never get finished at this rate unless everyone who could still work did overtime.

Andros must have been watching for them, because as soon as she pulled up in front of the clinic, he strode out of the door and helped Becka inside, Laurel following.

"You can come along if you want, or you can stay in the waiting room," he said, speaking to Laurel over his shoulder.

"I'll come." If Becka was anything like Laurel's sisters, she'd want someone by her side. They might believe they were all grown-up, but inside they still needed someone to turn to for comfort.

Laurel's chest felt heavy when the memories unexpectedly bombarded her. She'd been Becka's age exactly when she'd fallen into the dark hole of grief her parents' deaths had left her and her sisters with. All those summers she'd been stuck home watching her sisters while her parents were working had seemed hard. Then she'd learned that had been nothing compared to what it felt like for that comforting support to be forever gone.

"After I take a look, I'll have to thoroughly wash it out, okay?" Andros settled Becka by a low sink that was really more like an open shower, before his eyes met Laurel's. "Christina's not here right now. Want to help me get some supplies?"

"Of course."

She followed him into an exam room, and he pulled gauze, pads and a bottle of some liquid from a closet, handing them to her. "Were you with her when it happened?" he asked as he grabbed some sealed bags of what looked like syringes and suture kits and who knew what.

"Yes. It's a long, pretty deep gash. Not sure exactly how deep, but it bled a lot."

"What did you do for it?"

"Tried to bring the edges of the wound together, then pressed on it a while to stop the bleeding. Seemed to work well enough, then I bandaged it and brought her here."

"Sounds like maybe you should have forgotten about digging for a living and become a doctor."

Fascinated by that unexpected dimple that poked into one cheek as he paused to look at her, she nearly dropped the gauze and bottle and fumbled to hang on to them. "Since I feared I might pass out when I first saw all that blood, I think I chose the right career path."

"Think you'll faint if you watch me stitch it up?" he asked, a mischievous twinkle in his eyes. "If so, please stay in the waiting room. Last thing either of us needs is for you to keel over and crack open your beautiful head."

"I want to be there for Becka." She was aware of a deep feeling of relief that he obviously wasn't still irritated with her. Deeper than it should have been. And how ridiculous was it that him calling her head "beautiful" gave her a little glow inside as well? "Since I'm not responsible anymore for whether she lives or dies, I think I'll be okay."

He chuckled then instantly became all business when they walked into Becka's room and Andros pulled a rolling stool up next to her. "Let's take a look."

Laurel watched him carefully peel off the layers of gauze and wouldn't admit for the world that she had to look away a couple times when she saw the long, raw slice in Becka's calf that again oozed a trickle of blood.

"Nice first-aid job, Ms. Evans," he said, glancing up at her with a smile in his dark eyes. "I'm impressed."

"Thanks. Hope I don't have to do it again."

His eyes crinkled at the corners as he held her gaze for a moment, and darned if her heart didn't skip a beat before he turned to Becka. "I'm going to put a lidocaine-epinephrine mix all around the skin, then inject it with some painkillers before I wash it out. This part's going to hurt, I'm sorry to say."

Laurel and Becka both watched him gently but efficiently smooth on a liquid with a cotton pad, all around the edges of the torn skin. When he was done, he looked up at Becka, his dark eyes sympathetic. "Going to inject the painkiller into the wound now, which isn't going to feel good either. But then it'll be nice and numb when I stitch it up. Okay?"

Becka nodded, then gave a little crying gasp before she bit her lip hard as she had on the mountain. Laurel reached for the girl's hand, not sure if she was comforting Becka or both of them, again thinking of her own sisters and how upset she'd be if they were in pain like this. She remembered many small boo-boos when they'd smothered her with grateful hugs and kisses after she'd patched them up, managing to smile at the sweet memories.

She had to turn away a couple times as he repeatedly stuck the needle down into the open wound. "Will you think less of me if I say I'm glad my parents were archaeologists and didn't groom me to be a doctor instead?"

Andros glanced up at her with a smile. "Nothing would make me think less of you. And I have a feeling you'd be great at anything you put your mind to. Even medicine." He set aside the needle and vial, and attached a hose to the faucet.

"Thank God," Becka said fervently. "That was awful."

"I know. That's no fun, but you're doing great." He patted her knee. "Washing it out isn't a picnic either, so hang in there for me."

He hosed down the angry wound, washing it thoroughly as he'd done with Laurel's hand. She started to worry that poor Becka would bite right through her lip if she chomped on it any harder.

"When Dr. Drakoulias had to wash out the cut on my hand, I thought he might drain the entire Gulf of Corinth before he was done," she said, trying to distract the girl with a joke.

Becka managed a little laugh, thankfully. "Maybe then they wouldn't be able to catch any octopus to serve up at dinner, which Jason hounds me to eat every time. I can't get why he loves them. Doesn't he understand that those little suction cups weird me out?"

"Laurel thinks octopus suckers are a delicacy, don't you? Preferably washed down with ouzo." Andros's gaze lifted to hers for a brief moment, his dark eyes filled with that mischievous twinkle again as he winked.

"A delicacy if you're a whale or a Greek."

Andros grinned, and Becka laughed before the

sound morphed into a pained yelp. "Sorry. Not much longer."

Laurel sent up a prayer of thanks that the washing out was finally over, except the stitching would probably be an ordeal for the poor girl, too. Andros leaned back to pat Becka's shoulder this time. "The worst is over. Thankfully, right? The stitching is going to take a while because I need to do it in several layers. But believe it or not, it won't hurt at all."

"Find that hard to believe," Becka grumbled.

"Can't blame you. And I find it hard to believe you cut yourself this deeply with a trowel—that takes a special talent." He smiled, and that adorable dimple poked into his cheek as he began to stitch.

"Yeah, I have special talents all right. Clumsy ones."

His amused eyes met Laurel's and she found her heart beating a little harder for no reason at all. "I need to repair this cut in the muscle first, to stop it from bleeding, with stitches that will dissolve. Then the subcutaneous layer of flesh, which will reduce tension on the wound and help keep it closed and healing. Then, lastly, smaller nylon stitches that will help it look better when it heals."

"Jason said having a dig scar is a badge of honor," Becka said. "But if you can keep it from looking Frankenstein-ish, that would be great."

"Even though Laurel has no faith in the local, backwater Greek doctor, I promise no Frankenstein."

"I didn't say…oh, never mind." The amused teasing in the dark depths of his eyes told her an embarrassed protest was exactly what he'd been hoping for, and she wasn't going to go there again.

Laurel tried to keep up a bit of light conversation with Becka to take the girl's mind off her leg. Even while she was talking about the dig and asking things like what all the team had done in Delphi last night while she was out with Andros, she found her mind mostly on him.

Watching how smoothly, efficiently and impressively he stitched Becka's wound, obviously having done it hundreds of times. Noticing, as she had when he'd worked on her own hand, how dark his lashes were, how his features really were reminiscent of a classical Greek statue, how beautifully shaped his lips were as he slightly pursed them in concentration. Remembering how they'd felt against hers, which made her feel tingly and breathless and...and...

Stupid. Above and beyond any attraction she felt for the man, and there was no point in denying she had plenty, this dig came first. And with three team members in the hospital and Becka now likely out of commission for who knew how long, it was getting scarily harder to imagine she could make happen what she wanted to accomplish before they ran out of time.

She inhaled, willing her heart rate to pretend it wasn't thrown all out of whack just from his nearness. Time to bring business back to the forefront, get Becka to the hotel and herself back on the mountain.

"Since I forgot I was supposed to lure you to the mountain so you'd feel obligated to give us free medical care, I'll need a bill from you," she said.

"I'll have the office manager get it to you. I know US universities have insurance for teams like yours. And my yacht payment is due."

She tried hard to be immune to the power of his smile, but failed miserably. "Then why...?" Her voice trailed off. She'd been about to ask why he hadn't given her a bill for her hand, then wasn't sure she wanted to hear the answer. If it was because of this attraction that simmered between them despite her wishing it didn't, she didn't want to know. Having it verbalized instead of just zinging in the air around them might make it even harder to resist.

"You have a yacht?" Becka looked wide-eyed at him as he finished slathering on the same antibiotic he'd put on Laurel's hand.

"Well, a yacht by my standards, but probably not by Aristotle Onassis's." His eyes were focused on wrapping Becka's leg with layers of gauze, a different gauze wrap and elastic bandage on top of it all. "It's a twenty-five-foot boat with a two-fifty-horsepower motor. Perfect to take you both octopus fishing on your day off."

Becka laughed, and Laurel wondered how in the world she was supposed to resist lusting after a Greek god who cared for his patients, seemed to be a good dad, had a delicious sense of humor and even more delicious mouth?

"Ready, Becka? Your leg feel okay?"

"I'm sure it'll hurt like crazy later, but right now it's nicely numb." She turned to Andros, who was scribbling on a pad. "Thanks a lot, Dr. Drakoulias."

"You're welcome. You'll need to get crutches to keep weight off it for a few days, and I have a couple prescriptions for you that you can fill either at the pharmacy next door, or in Delphi. Just—" The sound of his phone ringing interrupted him. He fished it from his pocket, and, glancing at it, frowned. "Excuse me a minute."

His serious expression sent a little jab of concern poking at Laurel's chest. She prayed it wasn't some bad news about the Wagners or John. That kick of concern heightened her awareness of him as she watched him stride from the room, his butt perfectly encased in his dress pants, his broad shoulders tugging the fabric of his shirt, his black hair catching the bright overhead light, making it gleam.

"Wow, Laurel," Becka said, turning to her with awe in her voice. "I didn't really see him very well at the caves when John was sick. He's, like, wow."

"Yeah. He is." Hadn't that pretty much been her first thought too? Even more so now that she knew how it felt to kiss him. Though she was going to stop thinking about that if it killed her.

"Anybody could tell he's attracted to you. If you don't go for that, you're crazy."

Oh, yeah, she wanted to go for "that." It might be crazy not to, but it would be just as crazy to get into a quickie relationship right now. Except every time she was around the man, her resolve to keep her distance seemed to disintegrate, and kissing him became the forefront thought in her head. Maybe Ate, the spirit of mischief, was lurking on this mountain, luring her into infatuation and recklessness.

The thought made her smile, thinking of how her sisters always rolled their eyes when she said things like that, as though mythical beings just might be real after all. "This dig is important to me, Becka." No one but the Wagners knew exactly how important. "I admit I'm tempted. Really tempted. But I just don't have time, and we'll be out of here in a few weeks."

"Yeah, I know. But still, you could—"

They both turned to the door as Andros walked back in, his expression seeming lighter, yet at the same time hard to read.

"That was Dr. Dimitri Galanos. He has interesting news."

Laurel stood and moved next to him, practically holding her breath. "What news?"

"First, John is unfortunately still on the ventilator, though they're taking good care of him. But the Wagners continue to improve, and their test results are back."

"And?"

"It's apparently some type of virus, though they're still not sure what." His eyes met Laurel's. "However, it's definitely not a fungal infection. So it appears they didn't get it from the caves."

CHAPTER SEVEN

"So if it's not a fungal infection, why do you still have that look on your face? I thought—" Taryn interrupted herself to tug her son's shirt as he stood on his chair. "Petros, sit down, please, and play your game. Lunch will be here soon."

"What look?" Andros rebooted the tablet his wriggling daughter held, pulled up a new game to occupy Petros, then gave his attention back to Taryn. "This is why we should've just cleaned your fridge out and eaten leftovers. Our children are monsters when we go out."

"Not monsters, Daddy! Fairies!"

"Uh-uh! I'm a monster, Uncle Andros!"

Both their protests and dark frowns were so indignant, he had to laugh. "Okay, an impatient ants-in-her-pants fairy, and a messy monster. Have another olive."

He handed both the kids olives. He watched his daughter pop it into her mouth, then fish the pit out with her small fingers, filled all over again with amazement that she belonged to him. His own flesh and blood in the adorable little package that was Cassandra Anne Drakoulias.

It hadn't been the way he'd expected to start a family someday. Making a baby with a woman he hardly remembered, and who hadn't felt a need to tell him about his own daughter. If Alison hadn't died, he might *never* have known. That tore at his heart and sent the guilt of how carelessly he'd lived his life even deeper into his bones.

But from the very first instant he'd met his child, he'd realized what an incredible blessing she was. God's way of helping him rethink how he lived his life when he hadn't even realized he needed to.

"Mom would be horrified if we ate leftovers after church. She'd hop the next plane from Scotland and be fixing her usual massive feast for us like she does every Sunday. And scold me for not spending the day cooking."

He chuckled, because it was true. "She'd be almost as horrified to see us in a restaurant. Good news is she will never know, and she'll be back to cook and fuss over us in no time. In fact, I'm dying for her *avgolemono* soup, which you refuse to fix for me."

"Fix it for yourself." His sister smirked, because she knew his cooking skills were practically nil. Something he should probably work on. "Anyway, tell me why you're still frowning and deep in thought about the pneumonia," she said, bringing back the original subject, as usual. Once his sister had something she wanted to talk about, she was going to finish no matter what. "It's not a fungal infection, so it's not from the archaeological dig, and not something the workers are going to spread around town. Right?"

"We may know what it isn't, but we don't know what it is. Maybe they were just in the wrong place at the wrong time and sat next to somebody who passed it on. But maybe it's something else."

"Like what?"

Exactly what was bothering him. "I don't know. Di doesn't know. But I have a strange gut feeling that this isn't over."

"I remember a lot of your gut feelings just being hunger pangs," his sister said.

"Which is why you should have let me eat your *pastitsio* instead of coming all the way to Delphi for lunch." He grinned, willing his brain to stop thinking about the mystery. Time would tell whether he was right or wrong, and he hoped like hell he was wrong.

"Daddy, it's your pretty friend who knows lots about fairies!" Cassie said excitedly, pointing to the doorway.

He looked up and his heart gave a kick when he saw Laurel standing there with a few others from the dig, startlingly elegant in a long blue dress that skimmed her ankles and loosely hugged her curves. Elegant, and at the same time natural, with her beautiful hair in that thick ponytail she always wore it in, and little makeup on her exotic features.

Almost as though she felt his eyes on her, her gaze lifted to his and held, her lush lips parted in surprise until someone jabbed her arm and she turned to follow the host to their table. He had the urge to catch up with her, talk her into having lunch with them, but stopped himself. He knew a number of people in this place, and it wouldn't take much for elbows to nudge and knowing smiles and winks to be sent his way, starting gossip that no longer applied now that he had Cassie to think about.

"Can we ask her to eat with us, Daddy?"

Was his daughter a mind reader now? "Looks like she's eating with the dig crew, so let's not bother her."

"I won't bother her. I just want to ask a couple things."

Before he even realized what she was doing, Cassie slid from the chair and ran across the room to Laurel's table, with Petros following on her heels. "Cassie, you—ah, hell."

"Why 'ah, hell'?" His sister tipped her head at him with a quizzical look. "Seemed like she likes kids when I met her. She have the hots for you? Or is it mutual?"

"Why either one of those? Maybe we dislike each other."

"Yeah, right." His sister gave an indelicate snort. "I've never known a single girl to meet you and not be interested. And for the record, I've seen the way you look at her."

"I'm looking at her as someone connected to my patients. I'm building my reputation as an upstanding doctor and all-around good dad. Not looking for a woman."

"Uh-huh. Tell that to someone who doesn't know you that well. I'm well aware you have the occasional fling when you go out of town."

"I'm not a monk, but I only see a woman when I'm sure she just wants a fling too." He'd obviously have to try harder to keep his attraction to Laurel hidden. At least his sister couldn't see inside his brain as well, because she'd also learn that Laurel featured front and center in any number of fantasies at the moment. Then Taryn would laugh and shake her head and point out that there'd always been someone featured in his fantasies, and he'd have to point out—again—that was the old Andros, not the new, improved one.

"And of course I like to look at her," he continued. "She's a beautiful woman. But she's only here for a few weeks, and having some short thing with her wouldn't be worth the whole town gossiping about me and Cassie hearing it."

"So when are you going to give a relationship a chance to grow into something bigger than a fling?"

"You know as well as I do that I'm not capable of that kind of relationship."

"I don't believe that. Just because you used to go through women like Thea Stella goes through tissues, doesn't mean you can't have a long-term relationship. The lines to become Mrs. Andros Drakoulias started forming when you were about fifteen."

"I think you have to want one to have one."

"Maybe you just never met the right woman."

"Glad you have faith in me, but everyone in this town thinks different."

"People will always talk. I know I'm still on the subject list, having Petros without a wedding ring or a man who wanted to be involved in his life." His sister sighed. "So what if you were a bit of a playboy back in the day and gave the town some entertainment? That was a long time ago."

"Showing up in town with a two-year-old, shocking the hell out of everyone, wasn't all that long ago." After the phone call from Alison's brother, telling him about Cassie, the direction of his life had changed. Thankfully no one in Alison's family could take his little girl, or he might still not have her in his life. That second, he'd known becoming a more responsible man and moving to Kastorini with his daughter was his destiny, despite having to deal with the perennial tongue waggers. "One of these days, though, the past will be forgotten, if I behave myself."

"You never cared about the gossip before and you shouldn't now."

He glanced over at his daughter, talking animatedly to everyone at Laurel's table. "I have Cassie to think about."

"And I have Petros. We can flaunt our heathen ways together."

"We've always been experts at that." He had to grin. "How about we flaunt our newfound upstanding citizenship equally well?" The waiter brought their food, and Andros stood. "I'll get the kids."

He took one step and saw that Laurel was already headed their way, Cassie and Petros on either side of her, holding her hands.

"Lose something?" She smiled at Taryn before her eyes met his. Until he realized the moment went on a little too long and he quickly shifted his attention to Cassie.

"I did. My little fairy flitted away as soon as she saw you come in."

"And my monster followed," Taryn said.

"I asked Laurel if she'd come see our fairy house and tell us how we can get the fairies to move in."

A flood of instant pleasure filled Andros at the thought of her coming to Kastorini, spending time with him that afternoon at his home, while at the same time knowing it wasn't the best idea. "Miss Laurel probably has things she needs to do, Cassie."

"It's Sunday. Sunday is for playing," Cassie said, that cute frown on her face again. He had to smile, reaching out to smooth her brow with his fingers.

"True. But Miss Laurel may already have plans for how she wants to play today."

The second the words were out of his mouth, he knew exactly how he'd like to play with Laurel. His eyes met hers, and damned if his thoughts weren't reflected right back at him.

"At the risk of Cassie scolding me, I do have work to do today, since we're behind schedule," Laurel said, breaking the heated eye contact that somehow happened between them again. She looked down at his daughter. "But I'd enjoy stopping by for a short time to see your house and give a fairy-attracting consultation. It's the least I can do since your dad fixed up my hand for me."

"Speaking of which, I want to look at it again," Andros said.

"Thanks, but it's healing nicely."

"How did you get your boo-boo?" Cassie lifted up the hand she was holding, still wrapped in a bandage, and examined it with an interest that made Andros smile again. Who knew? Maybe his girl would become a doctor one day, carrying on the family tradition.

"I stabbed it with a potsherd. That's a piece of pottery that's broken, and we try to find all the pieces so we can put it back together again."

"I'm glad my daddy fixed it for you. He's a good fixer."

"Yes, I've seen that he is." She looked at him again, and the warm admiration in her eyes had him wondering what she saw in his own. "Your food's going to get cold. You go ahead and eat and I'll come down at, what, two o'clock?"

"Park at the clinic, and I'll meet you there. We'll walk around town some and I'll fill you in on a little of its history on the way to our house."

"I'll be there." She patted both children on their

heads and walked back to her table, her rear end gorgeously round and sexy in that clingy skirt of hers as she moved across the room.

Pretty oblivious to his lunch as he chewed, he became aware of Cassie jabbing her knife into the meat on her plate, and he quickly cut it for her as his sister softly laughed.

"What?" Though he damned well knew what. That it had been written all over his face, which he'd have to better control when Laurel came to town.

"Looking at her as someone connected to your patients?" Taryn's eyes gleamed with amusement. "Right. More like dessert."

"I want dessert, Mommy. Something really sweet," Petros said.

"Like uncle, like nephew." She chuckled, still looking at Andros with that sisterly smirk firmly in place. "Which means Kastorini's female population has much to fear in another ten years, Petros. Or much to look forward to, depending on your point of view."

Glad that Christina was on call for the clinic, Andros caught up on paperwork in his office.

Not very efficiently, though, since he kept seeing Laurel's beautiful face and shapely body in that dress of hers that made him want to skim his hands along its fluid lines. Feel her curves beneath it. Kept interrupting his work and thoughts to walk to the clinic's big front window to see if she had arrived.

Since when did he act like a smitten schoolboy in the throes of his first crush? That first crush was so long ago he could barely recall it, probably because it had been followed by plenty of others before he'd left for school in the US. Even more after he'd arrived there, where the world, and the number of women in it, got a whole lot bigger than his hometown of seven thousand people.

So why had Laurel gotten so thoroughly under his skin, making him feel so oddly restless and itchy? Could it be because he'd spent the past two years showing he was a reformed man? Somehow, he didn't think so. There was some intangible thing about her that, for whatever reason, just called to him like some irresistible siren.

About to go back to his desk, or, more accurately, the desk he shared with his father, he spotted her dusty sedan on the road that rounded the steep curve beyond the bell tower.

And just like that, his chest felt light, his work and the mysterious virus forgotten, his restlessness replaced by focus. On her.

With a sudden pep in his step, he went outside, locking the clinic door behind him. The car nosed into one of the empty parking spaces, and the smile on Laurel's face seemed as carefree as he knew his own was.

He leaned in through the car's open window. "Are you Laurel Evans, fairy consultant?"

"I am." Her beautiful smile made his own widen. "And my fee for attracting fairies is very reasonable."

"What is your fee?"

"I'm still deciding."

The way she looked at him, her eyes a brilliant, sweet, hot blue, practically melted him where he stood, and he struggled against the urge to grab her up, sit in the driver's seat and pull her onto his lap to help her decide real quickly about that fee. Show he was ready and willing to pay up however she wanted him to.

Attracting fairies? Hell, if she attracted them

as easily as she attracted him, his house would be overrun with the little things. He leaned closer to her in the hot car, a breath's distance away, her sweet, citrusy scent intensified by the heat of her body. "How long will it take to decide?"

"Hard to say, but I've learned to go with a gut feeling when I get one."

The breath rushed from his lungs and his heart bumped around in some off-kilter rhythm at her words. He knew exactly what he wanted, and from the way she was looking at him, she just might want the same thing. And how was he supposed to resist kissing her to find out? The question flitted into his mind, then promptly right out as, unable to think anymore, he closed the gap between them and kissed her.

Her mouth opened to his, moving, tasting, exploring in an excruciatingly slow dance that weakened his knees. Her kiss was sweet and hot and beyond irresistible. He cupped her cheek in his hand, stroking the fine bones there, the softness of her skin and wisps of hair adding another layer to the overwhelming sensual pleasure. He could feel her response, taste the small breathy gasps that touched his moist lips and sent him deepening the kiss until the loud, grumbling chug of a truck engine cut through his foggy brain.

He pulled his mouth from hers, barely aware of the truck disappearing with a cloud of black smoke puffing behind. Laurel's eyes were half-closed, her lips parted, their panting breaths sounding nearly as loud in the car as the truck had.

A jabbing against his ribs made him realize his torso was just about completely inside her car. He inhaled to catch his breath and clear his mind, thunking his head on the door frame as he extricated himself. A brain shake was probably something he badly needed.

"Ooh." She winced, scrunching up her face in that cute way she had. "That hurt?"

"No." Not nearly as much as stopping kissing her had. Which proved again that the woman was a siren, attracting him with her song and smile until he quit looking where he was headed, crashing on the rocks for all the world to see.

Hadn't he promised himself not to give the town any new gossip material? While getting it on with Laurel was about all he could think of at that moment, in a few weeks she'd be gone. If Cassie had to hear yakking about what a playboy her father still was, asking questions he didn't want to answer to a four-year-old, he'd hate himself for his weakness.

"Just leave your car here." He turned away from the question in her eyes, opening the car door and grasping her elbow with the hope anyone watching would just see it as a cordial gesture. "I'll be your Kastorini tour guide."

"Are you as good a tour guide as you are a doctor?"

"Not sure. You'll have to let me know if I'm good."

The heat and humor that sparked in her eyes made him think of that mind-blowing kiss, shortening his breath all over again. He wondered why he'd said it that way. Must be his subconscious thinking about the crazy chemistry between them.

Strolling the streets with her next to him felt strangely natural and right. Just as he'd felt after they'd been at the hospital in Vlychosia, reaching to hold her hand seemed a lot more normal than resisting it, which he managed only with extreme effort. The air around and between them held an odd tension, an intense awareness, that crackling spark he always felt around her. But at the same time he felt relaxed and comfortable as he told her about the various landmarks in town.

That relaxation diminished when he realized he could feel the curious stares fixed on them from houses they passed and from second-story windows of homes above the various shops. From the grinning men sitting at tables outside tavernas, drinking coffee or something stronger as they heatedly discussed whatever was the subject of the day, and enjoyed watching and talking about anyone who walked by while they were doing it.

He glanced at Laurel and could see she was aware of it too. "Living in a small town is a bit different from living in a big city. Didn't think I'd come back here because of it."

"But here you are." She looked up at him, one blond eyebrow quirked. "So why did you? Aside from the obvious charm of the place?"

She thought it was charming to be stared at? Or was she able to look beyond that to see the generations of history and how it connected all of them in a strong bond of community you couldn't find in a big city?

"Just decided it was time to come back. Take

my place as town doctor beside my father." No need to tell her the whole story. How he'd never been sure he wanted that for a lot of reasons, including the embarrassment his parents felt from his actions, and his sister's too. But the sudden situation with Cassie had shown him he needed it.

"Your father is a doctor too? Why haven't I met him?"

"He and my mother have taken advantage of me being back. They're traveling around Great Britain at the moment. Were supposed to come back this week, but decided Ireland had to be added on to the itinerary."

"How long have you been back?"

"Two years. They've been to the States and Canada, on various European tours, and to Iceland since then, believe it or not."

"My parents also loved traveling," she said softly, her eyes instantly wistful and sad, as they had been last time she'd spoken of them. "Most of it for digs without us, but we did have a few great trips to national parks and Washington, DC, and other places they deemed too important for their girls to miss."

"Glad you have those memories with them."

Now that he had Cassie, he couldn't imagine leaving her all summer every year, and wondered why Laurel's parents hadn't found a way to take their daughters with them. He let his arm slide around her shoulders to give her a brief, gentle hug. If he couldn't comfort someone in need, then to hell with those watching who might want to make something of it.

"I can see you give Cassie a lot of your time," she said, looking up at him with eyes that weren't quite so sad now. "That you're a good dad."

"I try to be." Wanted to be. And her words were a reminder, again, of why he shouldn't pursue the short but doubtless incredibly sweet time he knew he and Laurel could spend together before she left. "Thanks. Not sure that's always true, but I'm working on it." Working on it damned hard, if resisting the urge to touch her and kiss her counted. He shoved his hands in his pockets. "So here's the edge of town. The stone walls were built all the way down to the beach, complete with small angled cannon openings in the walls to defend against whoever wasn't in possession of the town and fortress at that moment."

"Is that a mosque? It doesn't look like a Greek church."

"It was. Built during Turkish rule. Later used as a schoolhouse, then a taverna, and now it's owned by someone who lives in Athens and comes to stay here occasionally."

He drew her to the outer wall to look down, where its smooth stones ended at the beach far below and swimmers lounged on large, flat rocks tossed among the boulders and slapped by gentle waves. Farther down, colorful fishing boats bobbed at the long wooden dock. "Kastorini never had the same height advantage a lot of walled cities had during the Ottoman Empire, built way up at the top of a mountain, but we had other things going for us. Back in the day, citizens could see any approaching ships from far away on the gulf, and the mountain behind is so steep and prone to rock falls that it was pretty hard for invaders to sneak up on us."

"So your ancestors were likely a mix of Ottomans and Venetians, with a little Byzantine and Turkish spice thrown in with salt and pepper. You're like a finely flavored Greek stew."

"That's very poetic. Greek mutt's probably more accurate."

Her soft laughter, the sparkle in her eyes, filled him with pleasure, and, while he didn't wrap his arm around her again as he wanted to, he moved closer until their shoulders touched.

"This place is just beautiful," she said, gazing around at the curving, narrow streets, the old homes, the arches covered with masses of vivid flowers, her expression warm and admiring. She shifted her attention to the gulf waters and the misty mountains beyond. "It's no wonder you wanted to come back."

"There was a time when I didn't want to. Now that's hard for me to imagine."

"I'm just starting my journey as an archaeologist, ready to travel all over. But I'd be lying if I didn't say it's awfully appealing to think of getting to live here forever. Someday, when I'm ready, I think I'll look to settle in a place like this."

They stood there together for what felt like long, peaceful minutes, watching the brightly colored fishing boats and a large tour boat slice through the sapphire waters of the Gulf of Corinth. Her scent, sweetly mingling with the tumble of flowers nearby, wafted to his nose again. It reminded him of their kiss, how she'd smelled and tasted, and the memory of that sensory overload nearly had him turning to her to do it again.

He curled his fingers into his palms, trying to focus his attention on the boats below. Just as he was about to suggest they move on, she turned to him. "Must be incredible to have this kind of history be a part of who you are," she said. "Studying it, loving it and being drawn to it like I am isn't the same as being a part of it."

"I guess it is. Like anything, you take it for granted sometimes until you're reminded of it." He looked down at her, saw the sincerity in her eyes. Eyes a color close to the mesmerizing blue of the gulf. "You ready to go stir up some Greek fairies?"

"Ready. And I think you've already paid my fee in full, Dr. Tour Guide."

He wasn't going to ask if she meant the tour, or the kiss. And if it was the kiss, he'd be happy to go deep into debt. "Our place is down this street just a short way. Watch your step. These cobblestones will trip you up if you're not—"

"Andronikos!"

Ah, hell. He turned to see his aunt laboring up the street parallel to his. What was she doing in this part of town? "Good afternoon, Thea Stella."

"*Kalispera* to you as well." She folded her arms across her ample bosom and stared at Laurel. "Who's the girl and what's she doing here?"

Always polite, his *thea*. Not. At least she'd spoken Greek, so Laurel wouldn't understand the words. "This is Laurel Evans, from the archaeological dig near Delphi. Laurel, this is my aunt, Stella Chronis."

"Nice to meet you." Laurel extended her hand with a smile, but his aunt just stared suspiciously.

"Hmph. A very pretty one, as usual, Andronikos." His aunt turned dismissively from Laurel, and the rudeness of it nearly had him pointing it out to the woman. Probably best to grit his teeth, though, since Laurel might not have thought much of it, and any comment would just call even more attention to her actions. At least she continued to speak in English instead of completely excluding Laurel from the conversation. "My friend Soula's nephew wants to meet you to talk about medical school."

"I'd be happy to."

"Good. And while you're at it, tell him about your foolish mistakes and how to keep his pants on, Andronikos. Like you are finally doing now." Frowning, she glanced at Laurel. "I hope."

He'd thought he was too old to feel embarrassed about much anymore, but now knew that wasn't true. If only she'd kept speaking in Greek, after all.

Any chance Laurel might be oblivious to what his aunt was referring to? He glanced at her and saw a small smile on her face. Since Stella was as subtle as a sledgehammer, he knew she'd probably figure it out. With his aunt's brows still lowered into a near scowl, she grabbed his face and gave him a kiss on each cheek before trudging up the steep road without a backward glance.

"Andronikos? Is that your full name?" Laurel tilted her head at him as they resumed walking toward his house.

"Yes, after my grandfather. Quite a mouthful. My aunts and mother are the only ones who use it."

"I like it. Andros for warrior and Nike for victory. It suits you."

"You think?"

"I do think." Her beautiful lips curved wider. "So does your aunt feel a need to protect you from women on the hunt?"

So much for hoping she wasn't listening. "Or women from me, maybe. I had a bit of a reputation as a young man. Sorry she was rude to you, but don't take it personally. Stella enjoys being rude to everyone."

"And here I was feeling special."

He had to laugh at that, enjoying the teasing smile in her eyes, glad she wasn't hypersensitive, or thinking less of him after his aunt's remarks. "You are, believe me. I knew that the first day I met you, and you were so stubborn about me treating your hand."

"Stubbornness is a special trait?"

"Never knew I found it attractive until I met you. But combined with beauty, brains and your unique brand of humor? Oh, yeah."

The eyes that met his had a twinkle in them but seemed to be searching too. She didn't have to look hard to see he had a major jones for her, and he didn't know what the hell to do about it, since it appeared to be mutual. Maybe some intimate time together far away from Kastorini or Delphi would burn it out, since that was pretty much his MO anyway. Laurel was leaving soon, so she wouldn't want more than that either, and just thinking about all that made his pulse quicken. "So there's my house, on the right with the—"

"Daddy! Laurel!"

Just as it had every day for the past two years, his heart warmed at the sight of his daughter tearing up the road to meet them, hair and arms flying, leaving the front door wide open behind her. It warmed even more when she flung herself at him, as though it had been days instead of hours since they'd been together.

"Koukla mou." He swung her into his arms, smiling at the excitement in her eyes, wondering how he'd gotten so incredibly lucky to have a daughter with such a sunny, happy nature. "What have you been up to since lunch?"

"Trouble with a capital T."

He heard Laurel laugh, and grinned. "Her usual answer. Gets it from her *papou*. I have a bad feeling that's going to be her answer for the next fifteen years, which strikes fear into her father's heart."

"Don't be scared, Daddy. I'm just kidding!"

She wriggled from his arms and grabbed Laurel's hand. "Come on. I want to show you my fairy house."

"Cassie, let's be polite and offer Miss Laurel something to drink first. Didn't your Thea Taryn make lemonade this morning? Let's go inside and ask her for some."

"She's out back with Petros, kicking the football."

"I don't think I can wait that long to see the fairy house, Andros. Mind if we have some after?"

"It's here." Cassie tugged Laurel to the side of the house where a small strip of dirt contained various flowers his mother planted and tended for him.

"These flowers are so pretty!" Laurel turned to him. "Are you a gardener?"

"Can't tell a weed from a flower. When I bought the house, my mother couldn't stand the weedy scrub and planted them."

"My *yiayia* is good with flowers," Cassie said. "She lets me help her grow them."

"I don't know much about flowers, Cassie. Maybe you could teach me some things."

His daughter beamed at the suggestion, pointing

at various blooms as she said some plant names. Andros had a feeling she might just be making them up as she went along, and his chest filled with warmth all over again as he looked from her to the woman sniffing blooms and asking questions, pretending she thought Cassie really was an expert.

Laurel's face was lit with a smile as bright as Cassie's, and he could see she'd been an amazing big sister. A sister who'd had to take on becoming their mother. How hard must that have been for her?

"It's good you have your fairy house tucked in among your *yiayia*'s flowers, Cassie. You probably know fairies love flowers. You know what else? They love olive wood too. I found this piece of wood that looks just like a little bed, don't you think?" Laurel pulled it from her purse and Cassie reached for it in awe. "I bet if we find something soft for a mattress, and put a flower petal or pretty leaf on it for a blanket, a fairy will love to come snuggle on it."

"Do you think fairies probably live in the olive groves, then?"

"I bet they do. I bet they're really close by, just waiting for a nice bed inside this nice house."

Seeing the two of them standing close together in front of his home, Cassie plucking flower petals, gave him a strange feeling. Just as he was trying to figure out exactly what it was, a cacophony of voices made him turn. Then stare.

What the hell? Two men were striding fast down the street, one carrying a microphone, the other following with a big camera on his shoulder. Numerous townsfolk were gathered around them, walking, talking and gesturing. Pointing right at him.

"Dr. Drakoulias? Doctor, we've been told there's a mysterious illness in Delphi, and patients came here to your clinic before they got so sick they had to be moved to the hospital in Vlychosia. Is it contagious? Are others in Delphi and here in Kastorini at risk?"

The guy shoved the microphone in his face, and he stepped back, not about to be railroaded into saying something that might trigger public hysteria. "We don't believe anyone is at risk. If you give me your contact information, I'll keep you informed as we know more."

The guy got annoyingly close, with the camera-man right behind him. "Does it have something to do with the archaeological dig? We talked to some of the people working there, and they said it might. And that the dig leader is here with you today." He shifted his attention behind Andros, craning to see around him. Anger swelled in his chest. He'd be damned if the man was going to harass Laurel and possibly scare Cassie.

"Again, I'll keep you informed."

The rude-as-hell jerk shoved past him and stuck the microphone in Laurel's alarmed face. Andros didn't even hear the questions the guy started bombarding her with, he just reacted with instinct. Stepped between them and went nearly nose to nose with him, ready to shove him away from her if he had to.

"Ms. Evans doesn't know any more than you do. Now get off my property." He turned to grasp Laurel's arm and Cassie's hand, hustling them both into the house and away from the media sharks he had a bad feeling had just begun their sniffing around for headline-grabbing blood in the water.

CHAPTER EIGHT

AFTER TALKING ABOUT the media mess with the dig crew for almost an hour, Laurel found herself tuning out the hubbub of conversation as they sat on the back deck of their hotel, darkness shrouding the misty mountains beyond.

How they could still be rehashing the afternoon's excitement with the media showing up to talk to each one of them, she didn't know. Lord knew she was beyond tired of talking about it. The shock of them showing up in front of Andros's house had faded, but she couldn't get out of her head the surprising expression on Andros's face when he'd stepped between her and that reporter. His hard-eyed, angry look and aggressive posture had her wondering if he might actually punch the irritating guy, and she was thankful he'd simply cleared them out of there before she'd had to say much.

Part of her had wanted to tell him she could

handle it, but the truth was she'd been all too glad he'd hustled her and Cassie away into his house. It hadn't occurred to her she might be asked about the sick crew members. Thanks heavens she had some time now to think of how she should answer.

The intrusion had ruined what had been an otherwise beautiful day. Spending time with adorable little Cassie had been even more fun than she'd expected, making her feel all warm and fuzzy inside. Helen had been twelve when their parents had died—about to start her teen years. Adorable in her own way, she'd been a little trying at times too. That might be true for Cassie as well, though she couldn't imagine the child being anything but cute as a button.

It struck her with surprise that Helen had been even younger than Cassie when their parents started spending entire summers, rather than just weeks, away. How had they been able to leave her that long? Later leaving all three under Laurel's insufficient care and guidance?

She didn't think she could do that if she ever had children of her own someday, no matter how much she loved her work. Then fiercely shook her head, feeling a bit like a traitor to judge her parents that way. Reminded herself of how they'd both explained they were showing their girls that family life had to be balanced with work life.

Reminded herself how important their work had been to both them and the archaeological world. Reminded herself it was just as important to her, which she'd nearly forgotten today as she enjoyed herself in Kastorini.

Would this sudden media circus create yet another distraction from the job they had to get done with fewer hands and little time? She'd reminded the crew they had to focus, and they'd all agreed. Still, she knew it was human nature to love being on camera and part of a medical mystery, despite worrying about Mel, Tom and John in the midst of it.

Restlessness overcame her, and she stood. "I'm going to my room to plan where everyone will be working tomorrow. Let's get an early start. Be at breakfast at seven a.m., please."

The nods and quick good-nights they sent her way were perfunctory as they kept up the steady yakking, and she shook her head, hoping it didn't continue tomorrow when they had to get digging instead.

In truth, she'd already planned out tomorrow's schedule and decided she needed some fresh air instead of a stuffy room. The street outside the hotel was so dark she could hardly see, and she paused, wondering what might calm this strange unease. Maybe just a long walk around the tiny town of Delphi, even a little mindless shopping she hadn't taken time to do much of, would be enough to help her refocus.

Every store owner competed for the summer tourists, staying open until midnight or later if a single customer was around. One or two shop-keepers stood in their doorways, enthusiastically promising her good prices if she'd just come in and look. Others were busy with customers who had likely earlier toured the ancient sites and the wonderful museum that held the incredibly mas-sive statues, friezes and sphinx. And of course, the stunning bronze Charioteer. That famous Del-phi antiquity just might be eclipsed if she could only locate the treasure her parents believed in.

The one they'd died trying to find.

Laurel gave her head another forceful shake and stepped into a jewelry store, wanting to rid herself of thoughts of death and tragedy, of failure and unfinished dreams. At the back of the store, she peered into one of the many open cases of jewelry. A silver necklace reminded her of the one she wore at that moment—the necklace her sisters had given her for her birthday a few years back.

She reached up to grasp it in her hand, glad to have something to think about that made her smile. The three of them had made a massive birthday cake for her, one that ended up flat on one side and such an ugly deep blue they'd all laughed themselves silly over it. But it had tasted good, and it had been a wonderful evening of sisterly togetherness. A lovely memory among so many special moments the four of them had had over the years. A lovely memory among some that were not quite so great. Memories of all the times she'd despaired over her lack of maturity and skill trying to raise them.

A pair of earrings caught her eye and she picked them up, wanting to look more closely at the silver swirls that curled around the stones, thinking they seemed similar to an ancient pattern on a bracelet they'd unearthed at the dig.

"Moonstones help protect you during your travels, I've heard," a deep voice said next to her ear.

"Maybe you should get those earrings, since you'll be moving on soon."

She turned to see Andros behind her, but of course she'd known it was him. Even if she hadn't recognized his voice, every nerve in her body had, tingling and quivery and instantly alert to his nearness. Just as they had been earlier in Kastorini, when flirting with him had been so much fun, even as she'd told herself she shouldn't. When touching and kissing him had been at the forefront of her mind even as she'd been fascinated by the history of the place.

"What are you doing here?"

"Hoping to find you. Wondered if the media had harassed you anymore."

"Thankfully, no. And I don't need the moonstones quite yet."

"I thought maybe that had changed. That maybe you'd be closing down the dig sooner rather than later."

"Why would I?" She stared into his eyes, dark and serious, with a touch of something else. Puzzlement? Frustration? "I'm here until the funding ends and the university tells me I have to leave."

"Do you really want to have to deal with all the

media questions now? They might not have followed you here tonight, but I promise they'll be
up on the mountain, hounding you."

"I can handle it. I'm not afraid of them. Speaking of which, while I appreciate the gesture, I
didn't need you to rescue me today." Didn't need
it, maybe, but hoped he didn't know how much
she'd been glad of it.

"I know you didn't. Just didn't want him scar-
ing Cassie."

The way his lips curved showed that was a lie,
and that he probably knew she'd been lying too.
She found herself smiling back. "Got to admit,
he was pretty scary."

"I do have one question."

"That sounds ominous."

"Why? Why don't you just be done with it, so
you don't have to worry about whether the illness
has to do with the dig or worry about the damned
reporters swarming around?" His hands moved
to cup her face, tilting it up as he moved closer,
practically torso to torso. "Surely after five years
of excavating here, it can't matter much one way
or the other if you close it down now or two weeks
from now."

"We don't know what amazing artifact we still might find, just like we don't know anything about Mel and Tom and John and why they got sick. I…okay, I can't deny it worries me. But since we don't know if it had anything to do with the dig, I can't justify completely closing it."

He just kept staring at her, and, despite the unsettling, irksome conversation, Laurel found she couldn't move away from his touch. From the heat of his chest so close to hers. Couldn't stop her gaze from slipping from his eyes to the oh-so-sensual shape of his lips and back. What was it about this man that shook up her libido so completely?

"Until I met you, I'd always figured archaeologists to be easygoing, steady academics who analyzed facts," he said.

"And the facts are…?"

"Three sick people with similar symptoms. Cause unknown."

"Those are pretty vague facts, if you could even call them that. I wouldn't have a chance at any kind of grant if I told them a dig site was kind of like another dig site, but I didn't really have any idea what might be found there or why."

His lips curved slightly again as he shook his

head. "Who knew your head was as hard as the rocks you've unearthed?"

"Is that a compliment?"

The smile spread to his eyes, banishing the deep seriousness, and Laurel found herself relaxing and smiling too, in spite of everything. She didn't want to have to defend herself and her decisions and her goals to anyone, least of all this man she couldn't deny sent a zing with a capital Z through every part of her body whenever he was near.

Like now. Very, very near.

His lips touched her forehead, lingered, and, surprised at the deep pleasure she felt from just that simple touch, Laurel let her eyes drift closed until he dropped his hands and drew back. "If you won't listen to logic, at least let me buy you the earrings. Maybe they'll help you remember Delphi, and keep you safe on your travels into that damned cave."

"Not a good idea."

"Why? You afraid I'll expect a thank-you kiss?"

His expression was teasing and serious at the same time, and at his mention of a kiss Laurel's gaze dropped right to his mouth. She wasn't sure she should tell him about moonstone lore, but just as she decided that would be a bad idea the words came out in a near whisper. "Because for thousands of years, people have believed moonstones are a channel for passion and love from the giver to the receiver. A talisman for secret love. Carnal love. Can't risk igniting the power of a moonstone, can we?"

The scorching blaze that instantly filled his eyes weakened her knees, so it was a good thing his strong hands grasped the sides of her waist, pulling her flush against him. Everything about him seemed hot—that look in his eyes, the breath feathering across her lips, every inch of his body touching hers.

"I don't know. Can we? Seems like something's ignited even without the stones."

Whew, boy. Her body answered, *Oh, yes, we can, and right now, please*, while her brain tried not to short-circuit any more than it already was. She opened her mouth to say something—what, she wasn't sure—when she realized the shopkeeper had come to stand next to them.

"Welcome, welcome. May I assist you?" he said in a loud, robust voice. "Would you like a price for one or more of our fine pieces of jewelry?"

They both turned, and Andros dropped his hands from her. She should have welcomed the interruption to help her gather her wits, but really wanted to tell the guy to go away so they could get back to the steamy conversation that made her breathless. "No, thank you," she said. "I was just looking."

"Mister? Surely you wish to buy the beautiful miss something as beautiful as she is. At the best prices, you understand."

"We're still deciding if it's worth the risk. Thanks anyway," Andros said, his lips quirking as he looked at her, but that barely contained blaze that still smoldered in his eyes had her quivering all over again.

The man looked perplexed at Andros's answer, and kept peppering them with questions and various offers as they made their way out of the store, shouting after them to be sure to return for 'the better price' than the original ones he'd been offering.

Andros's arm was around her back, her waist again cupped in his hand as they walked to the darkest end of the street. It curved around in a U-turn to the adjacent street full of more tavernas and shops, but Andros stopped next to a stone retaining wall, beneath tall, arching shrubs that grew from behind it.

He pulled her into his arms, flashing a smile that practically lit up the dark corner he'd finagled them to. "It's not helping, you know."

She had a pretty good idea what he was talking about, but said instead, "What's not helping?"

She could feel his hands splay open on her back, pressing her close, as his warm mouth touched her cheek, moved over to her ear, giving it a tiny lick. "Not having the moonstone. Don't need that to feel a powerful desire for you. To want to share some passion with you. I've been fighting it since the second I met you, but it's been a losing battle."

The low rumble of his voice, along with the little kisses he kept placing against her ear, her neck, her cheek, managed to narrow her entire universe down to those singular sensations. She let her hands slip up his wide chest, outlining his hard pectorals as she went, gratified to feel his muscles twitch and bunch beneath her touch.

She turned her face to give him access to her other cheek, because she liked the breathless feeling it gave her and wanted more of it. Apparently amused at that, he chuckled as he softly kissed every inch of sensitive skin on that side as well.

"I don't have time to…to get involved with you." Proud of herself that she'd managed to remember that, she tipped her head back as his tongue explored the hollow of her throat.

"I know. And I can't risk getting involved with you."

"Risk?" Risk? What did that mean?

"Never mind." His mouth moved in a shivery path up her throat until it was soft against her lips. "This isn't involvement, right? Just friendship."

That startled a little laugh out of her, and she felt his lips smile against hers. "Yes. Friendship with benefits."

And then he kissed her for real. Softly at first, then harder and deeper. Dizzy from the pleasure, she moved her hands up from his chest to cling to his shoulders. There were some firm, taut muscles right there, perfectly placed for her to hold on to so she could stay on her feet and not melt into a small hot puddle on the still-steamy blacktop.

One wide hand slid farther up her back to gently cup her nape, his warm fingers slipping into the hair against her scalp that had loosened a bit from her ponytail. She thought her heart might pound right out of her chest at the thrilling barrage of every sensation he'd managed to make her feel in a matter of minutes—hot, weak, strong and slightly delirious.

A sound of need came from one of them, a little moan from one moist mouth to the other, with an answering gasp in return. The kiss got a little wilder as he pressed her so close, she felt her body mold completely with his. In the foggy recesses of her brain, a bizarrely wild sound filled her ears, and for a moment she feared it had come from her. Then realized with relief that it hadn't, that, somehow, they were surrounded by a cacophony of cat meows.

Andros seemed unaffected, kissing her with a single-minded focus that weakened her knees all over again, until the crescendo of sound was so distracting, she was finally able to break the kiss to look around.

"What in the world is that?"

His eyes, glittering through the darkness, met hers with heat and humor. When he answered, the sound was breathless and amused. "Feral cats.

They're everywhere in Greece. Haven't you noticed?"

"They've stared at us and walked around while we ate dinner on the outdoor patios here, but I guess I didn't realize. Thought they were pets of the owners." Still caught close in his arms, she turned to the tangle of shrubs next to them, astonished to see a nearly uncountable number of eyes staring at them luminously through the darkness. Big, small, up close and hiding deeper in the greenery; she couldn't imagine how many there must be.

"Greeks have a love of animals. And also can turn a blind eye to their needs sometimes as well, unfortunately. But many do feed the strays, when they can." He loosened his hold on her to dig something from his pocket, tossing it to the cats, then tossing more of it deeper into the thicket. The mad scramble that ensued made Laurel's heart hurt for the poor hungry creatures.

"Are they never neutered?"

"Just by a few of us. Our secret, though."

She looked up at him, so impressed at his caring. At his warmth, which he'd now shown her extended to all creatures, great and small. "Our secret. Though I didn't know you had surgical skills, too."

"I have many mad skills you don't know about." Their eyes met and held, and it was all there, swirling between them. The intimate smiles, the banked-down heat, the connection that made her feel as if she knew the man so much better than she possibly could after only days.

Had she ever felt such a strange, sensual connection with any other man? As soon as the question came, she knew the answer.

Never.

"It's good that you help little creatures. Back at home, we—"

The harsh ring of his phone made them both jump. The instant he looked at its screen, a deep frown replaced every bit of the heat and humor that had been there before.

"Ah, hell." His gaze lasered in on hers for a moment before he took a few strides away to answer. "Di. What's the matter?"

The second she heard who it was, her gut clenched. The man wouldn't be calling on a Sunday night to catch up on the weather.

Her breath seemed to completely stop, and her

hands went cold as she watched his expression get grimmer with each passing second. Finally he turned to her, and she found herself praying.

"Andros. Please don't tell me…Mel and Tom…" She gulped, not able to finish the sentence.

He reached for her hands and held them tight. "It's John. They're doing everything they can, but Di felt we should know. He's taken a turn for the worse."

CHAPTER NINE

"JOHN IS SICKER?"

The blue eyes staring up at him were wide and worried. Her hands had tightened on his so hard, her short nails dug into his skin. "The breathing machine is having trouble compensating for the pneumonia in his lungs, getting him enough oxygen. But they're giving him the best care they can." He'd known John's condition was becoming more precarious but hadn't seen any reason to alarm her more than necessary.

"What about Mel and Tom?"

"They're getting better every day." He stroked her back, hoping to soothe. "They're going to be fine, and hopefully John will come around too."

"Thank God." Her stiff posture seemed to relax just a little and she dropped her head to his chest, wrapping her arms loosely around his back. "I have to tell everyone he's worse. I have to give them a choice about whether they want to work at the site anymore. I still can't imagine they got sick from the dig, for all the reasons we've talked about. But who knows?"

"Wouldn't it end your stress to just shut it down, like I said before? Let your people go on home? You wouldn't have to worry about someone else getting ill or the media badgering you."

"I can't this second. Have to think. I don't expect you to understand."

No, he didn't understand, but now wasn't the time to get on at her about it. Not when she was feeling so upset and anxious. "I'll come talk to your crew with you. Explain his condition and answer any more questions they might have."

"Thank you. I'd…I'd appreciate that."

She slipped from his hold in what seemed like slow motion, as though it was a supreme effort. He was glad she didn't feel she had to shoulder the entire burden of talking to everyone about John's health.

They walked back to the hotel, silent but for the sounds of their feet on the pavement, the breeze rustling leaves in the trees, the mewls from hidden cats. The hotel seemed equally silent, and Laurel led him through a few cavernous rooms toward a door that led to a deck. Through the floor-to-ceiling windows, it was obvious even in the low light that the deck was empty.

"When I left awhile ago, they were all back here." She nudged open the door, and he followed her outside. The deck spanned the distance along the entire back of the hotel, but the only visible people were a couple in an embrace at the far end.

"Maybe they went to a bar. Or to bed, since I told them we'd be getting an early start."

"You want me to come back in the morning to talk with them then?"

"That's sweet of you, but no." She shook her head. "It's part of my job, though if he's any better in the morning, I'd really appreciate it if you tell me early."

"I admire that you're serious about your job and your responsibilities. Taking care of your sisters." He reached for her, stroked his hands up and down her soft arms. Soft, yet strong, just like her. "You step up to any task forced on you, no matter how difficult."

"Doesn't everybody?"

"No." Quite a few had doubted he could step

up when he'd found out about Cassie. "You have a lot to be proud of, Laurel."

The eyes that lifted to his were somber. "Not enough. Not yet."

He wondered what she meant, but when he opened his mouth to ask, got sidetracked completely when she suddenly twined her arms around his neck, pressed her soft curves against him. Pressed her sweet mouth to his.

Her lips plied his, gentle yet insistent. A controlled kiss, but with a slight desperation to it he knew came from her fears for the Wagners, the stress of the dig, the worry of John's worsening illness. Of her parents' deaths just a mile from where they stood. He could sense all of it, feel all of it, as though their hearts and minds had melded together along with their lips, and he hurt for her. Wanted to erase some of that hurt as best he could.

He let his hands roam down her back, to the curve of her waist, found them sliding farther south to grasp the round, firm globes of her rear, pressing her against his hardness. He'd wanted to touch her like this, hold her like this, every time they'd been near to one another, every time they'd kissed. The feel of her was everything he'd known it would be, and it was all he could do to not let his hands explore more of her. Tug the straps of her dress down her arms to cup the small mounds beneath, learn their sweet shape. Help her forget anything but this moment.

Her fingers slid to the sides of his neck, into his hair, making him shiver, sending his pulse ratcheting even higher. He knew he had to get control of himself before he lowered her into one of the deck chairs and made love to her right there under the stars.

It took Herculean effort to pull his mouth from hers and suck in a deep breath. "Don't think either of us wants to be caught out here by your dig crew or, God forbid, somebody working at this hotel who lives in Kastorini. Or, best of all, media types back for another interview and photo op." And wasn't that a hell of an understatement?

"Then let's go to my room."

His heart jolted hard at her words at the same time every muscle in his body tightened, ready to grab her hand and head there at a dead run. "Laurel. I want you. Which I'm sure you know. But not when you're hurting. Not when you might regret it tomorrow."

"I won't regret it. Just tonight. Just this once." She cupped his face in her hands. "I can't let myself be distracted from what has to get done at the dig. But right this minute I don't want to think, I just want to feel. Not feel alone, but feel good. With you. Which, if I'm honest, I've wanted to do since we first met."

"Laurel." His hands tightened on her behind, which pressed her pelvis tighter against him. He nearly groaned. All he wanted was to make her feel good. But would he be taking advantage of a weak moment? The same way he'd often thoughtlessly done, not all that long ago?

"Andros." There was a flicker of slightly amused impatience in her eyes when she said his name in return. Her hands slipped to his chest as she took a half step back. "I'm not a wilting violet you need to look out for or worry about, if that's the problem. I'm strong, and I've been on my own a long time now. You have about five seconds to say, 'yes, that sounds great' or 'no, thanks.' So which is it?"

A surprised chuckle escaped him. The woman standing in front of him definitely wasn't a needy, weepy, sad soul. She was fire and light, toughness and softness, and he was the luckiest man alive that she wanted to be with him tonight.

"Yes, that sounds great."

Her response was to grasp his hand and tug him along behind her through the foyer, up three flights of stairs and into a tiny room. He shut the door behind him and leaned against it, wanting to give her one more chance to change her mind. One more moment to decide if this was really what she wanted tonight.

When she turned to him, the desire that shone in her eyes reflected his own. He took a deliberate step toward her, keeping it slow and easy, giving her just a little more time. A little more space.

"Something about the way you're moving toward me reminds me of a lion on the hunt," she said, taking an equally slow step as the gap between them closed from four feet to three.

"And something about the way you're moving makes me think of a siren. Sending me out of my mind. Making me crazy. Which has occurred to me more than once, by the way."

"Has it?" Another step brought her close enough to touch. Her fingers reached for his shirt buttons, began flicking them open one by one, and his heart thudded thickly in his chest in response. "I never thought of being a siren, until I met you. What if I confessed that, the moment I saw you on the mountain, you made me think of a warrior god? Maybe even Apollo himself."

His laugh morphed into a low moan as her hands slid across his skin to spread open his shirt, her fingertips caressing his nipples. "Oh, yeah?"

"Yeah."

"I don't think I have much in common with Apollo."

"Are you sure? I can think of several things."

If his self-discipline hadn't already disintegrated, it would have at the way she was looking at him, smiling at him, touching him. "Such as? I'm not musical, never shot an arrow in my life and can't claim to be a prophet."

His stomach muscles hardened, along with notable other parts of his body, when her hands tracked down his skin to unbutton his pants. "You're a healer, right? Not to mention you seem to create heat and light whenever I'm around you. And as for physical beauty, you—"

"Okay, enough of this torture." He swept her hands aside, lifting his fingers to the thin straps of her dress. "Part of me wants to let you keep going, so I won't have to wonder if I'm taking advantage of you. But that concern is dwarfed by wanting to give you what you asked for." He slipped the straps down her arms. "Which is to just feel."

"Believe me, touching your skin is a good way for me to just feel."

"I have a better way. And can't wait another second to see *your* physical beauty, which I've fantasized about for days." He reached behind her, unzipped her dress. Slid it down the length of her body until it pooled at her feet, and he could see her luminous skin. He smiled at the paleness of her belly compared to her tanned arms and legs. Swept his fingertips across her stomach and over her white bra, lingering at her hardened nipples. "I like your archaeologist's version of a farmer's tan."

She gave a breathless laugh. "No time to sunbathe at the pool. Sorry."

"I love it. It's just like you. A woman of contrasts, all light and dark." He kissed her throat, moved his tongue down her delicate collarbone. "Soft." He slowly moved down over her bra to

take that tempting nipple into his mouth through
the fabric. "And hard."

Her hands grasped his head again, holding him
against her. He reveled in the little gasping sounds
she made as he moved from one breast to the
other, dropping to his knees to softly suck on her
belly. The scent of her arousal surrounded him,
so delicious he groaned as he pressed his mouth
over the silky fabric covering her mound, moist-
ening it even more.

"Come back...up here." Her voice was a little
hoarse as she grasped his arms, tugging.

He wanted to stay exactly where he was for a
while longer, but he was here to make her feel
good. Do what pleased her, what made her happy.
He stood and flicked off her bra, thumbed her
panties down her legs at the same time she shoved
his pants to his ankles. Kicking them off along
with his shoes, he took her into his arms and
kissed her, backing her toward the bed.

He broke the kiss to flick back the covers. When
he looked at her, standing there gloriously naked,
he realized there was one more thing he needed
to see. He reached around to her ponytail, gently
tugging at the elastic band there. "I want to see

your hair down. I want to see it spread over you, feel it touching my skin."

A sensuous smile curved her lips and she reached behind to pull off the band, dragging her fingers through her hair as she brought it over her shoulders to cover her breasts, her pink nipples peeking out of the silken strands.

He touched its softness, stroking from her ears down over her breasts, and could barely speak at how beautiful she was. "I've wondered how you'd look. It's better than any of my fantasies. Just like etchings of beautiful sirens rendering men helpless with one glance."

"I hope you're not helpless." She reached for him, and he picked her up to lay her on the bed. Touched her and kissed her, wanting to give her the pleasure she deserved.

The little sounds she made nearly drove him wild, and he lay on top of her to feel all of her skin against all of his. Then suddenly froze in horror.

"I don't have a condom." *Damn it to hell.* "But I can still make you feel good."

"Well, I, um, I bought some recently. Just in case, you know?" She looked at him with an adorably embarrassed expression before leaning over to rummage in her purse, handing him one. A breath of relief whooshed from his lungs.

"Smart, beautiful, responsible and even resourceful. A woman a man can only dream of." He took care of the condom as fast as possible, because he couldn't wait another second to join with her, holding her close, slipping inside her moist heat with a groan.

They moved together, their eyes locked, and the universe narrowed to that one moment, skin to skin, breath to breath, soul to soul. Seeing her lying there, her beautiful hair billowing all across the pillow, his name on her lips, sent him over the edge. Watching her eyes, darkened with bliss, hearing and seeing her fall with him, was a moment he knew he wouldn't forget if he lived a thousand years.

Laurel stared at the pastel pink-and-blue sky, the morning sun still low over the mountains beyond their Delphi hotel. How was it possible to have so many different balls of emotions rolling all around in her stomach at the same time?

Last night, she and Andros had been lying bonelessly sated and content, skin to skin and heart to heart, when his phone had rung. A call that had obliterated every ounce of pleasure, delivering the shocking, unbelievable news that John had passed away.

Her throat and eyes filled with tears as that terrible tragedy, that horrible reality, took precedence over everything. When she'd called a late meeting to somehow tell everyone about his tragic death, the horror on their faces had been every bit as intense as her own.

Those other balls rolling around were from grief and fear. Worry and anxiety. John's death likely wasn't connected to the dig, but it was still a terrible, heavy loss. A loss that added to her determination to finish what she'd come here to do. Finish the work her parents had died for. And now John too.

She swallowed hard at the sickly churning in her stomach as she waited for the dig crew to show up again. She'd asked them to meet with her again after breakfast to give them options. A breakfast she hadn't joined them for, since she doubted she could get one bite of food down anyway.

John. Dead. How was it possible? She still couldn't wrap her brain around it.

And was that going to be Mel and Tom's fate as well? "No," she said out loud, fiercely. Willing it to be true. Praying for it. Andros had promised her they would be fine.

Somehow, the thought calmed her stomach and helped her breathe slightly easier.

"Laurel. Are Mel and Tom…still okay?"

She looked up to see Becka hobble into the room on her crutches, looking pale and upset. Worried. As they all did, now filing quietly behind her to lower themselves into the mismatched crowd of overstuffed chairs and sofas, their faded fabrics showing varying degrees of wear.

"Yes, they're okay. Apparently anyway. Dr. Galanos told me they'll likely be released soon, which would be wonderful. I…I need to talk to them, find out what their plans are." Did their plans include coming back to the dig? Or going home? Certainly, after what they'd been through, no one could blame them for doing exactly that.

As she was interim team leader, the painful job of contacting John's family had fallen to Laurel. Tears welled in her throat again as she remembered their stunned silence, then bewildered and disbelieving questions. Then a near hysteria of grief and pain that had cracked her heart in two.

Did it make her weak and pitiful that she'd been beyond relieved to finally be done with her deliverance of the shocking news, passing the phone to Andros to further explain and try to comfort? Probably, yes. But with her own memories of receiving the nightmare call about her parents forever burned into her heart and mind, it was all she could do to maintain her composure. To not begin sobbing with them, which would have just made it all the worse for John's family.

Laurel drew in a deep breath, swallowed again at the threatening tears. She looked at the dig team—her team—perched or sprawled on the chairs, and realized two were missing. "Where are Jason and Sarah?"

"Jason's coming in a minute," Becka said. "He's feeling a little sick to his stomach. Because, you know..."

Becka's voice faded away as a few team members looked down at the floor. Yes, they all knew. Jason had become good friends with John over the past months, even though the college boy had been seven years younger than John. Almost like a big brother to the young man, Laurel supposed, and her chest pressed in even tighter at the thought.

"Sarah didn't answer her phone when I called to ask if she was ready," one of the girls said. "Probably still in the shower or something. Or maybe she, you know, needed a little more time to compose herself."

Laurel understood. She wished she had more time, too.

"Well, let's go ahead and get started." Laurel braced herself to ask what she had to ask. Knew their answers might well mean working with a thin crew, and she'd simply have to put in even more hours on her own. In fact, she might prefer that. No matter how much she wanted to find the artifact, she couldn't feel good about possibly putting others at risk for it.

"This is a devastating thing for all of us," she said. "John was not only an enthusiastic, hardworking person, he knew a lot about archaeology after volunteering on so many digs the past few years. We'll miss him as a friend. And we'll miss him as a teammate."

All eyes on her, they sat silently, two of the girls sniffing back tears. Laurel dug her fingers into her palms, kept her eyes away from the anguish on the girls' faces, and forged on. "No one knows why John died. What he had, or where he got it, or even if it could possibly have been contagious. If it was the same thing as the Wagners or not. Dr. Galanos said the hospital is working to find out, but we just don't have those answers yet. So I must give you all the option of deciding whether or not you still want to be part of this dig."

"I do," Becka said instantly. "If it was contagious, we'd already have been exposed anyway, right? I feel fine, and it seems to me everyone else does too. What's the point of quitting now, when we're so close to the end? I mean, I found those cool coins just last week, and the day before Sarah found those amazing ivory feet, just like the ones in the Delphi museum! Think what else we still might find!"

Becka's impassioned plea lifted the weight in Laurel's chest ever so slightly and she managed a smile. "Thank you, Becka. Though you have to take a few more days off until your leg has had time to heal. I'm not asking you all to decide this minute. I'll be working on the mountain as soon as we're done here, and possibly in the cave as well. Those who want to join me are welcome, so long as you understand there may be a risk involved, and you're willing to take that risk. Any of you end up deciding you want to pack it in and schedule flights home, I completely understand and support your decisions."

Just by watching them, seeing who made eye contact with whom and what expressions they wore, made it fairly easy to figure out who wanted to go and who would stay. And who could blame them? No matter how few hands would be left, though, she had to keep believing there was still a chance to finish what she had come to do.

"Talk it over with one another. Feel free to take the day off, then sleep on it," she advised them. "You can let me know in the morning, and we'll go from there."

As she looked at the uncertain faces, her whole body felt a little numb, but jittery and anxious as well, and she knew the antidote was work. Give them time and space without them feeling as if she was hovering around to coerce them, or judge them. Last thing she'd want would be for someone to stay on from guilt. Shorthanded or not, everyone still working tomorrow needed to feel as passionate about the project as Becka did.

"I'm heading up, if anyone wants to go. If you decide to come later, you'll find me at the mountain excavation first."

She swung up her day pack, and Becka followed her to the stairwell. "Let me tell Jason you're ready to leave. I'll be right back."

Laurel's lips twisted a little that the only person still for sure on board was handicapped with a bandaged-up leg and couldn't work for days. She closed her eyes and lifted her face skyward. "Any way you two know where it is? Don't angels have special powers? I need your help, here."

"You talking to the ceiling, or yourself?"

She opened her eyes to see the dark chocolate gaze of the man she'd gotten to know, oh so intimately the night before. They were serious eyes, questioning. As he walked across the wide foyer, bronzed and strong and so gorgeous, the utter male beauty of him stole her breath. That jittery nervousness in her stomach faded away to a feeling of warmth.

Which was dangerous. If this attraction had

been a distraction she couldn't afford before, she could afford it even less now.

"Just talking to my parents," she said, keeping her voice light so he wouldn't read too much into it. "Hoping for some divine intervention."

Sympathy joined the other emotions in his eyes as he came to stand in front of her. His hands stroked her arms, slowly, softly, soothingly as they had last night. "Find any?"

"No luck so far. Guess I'm on my own."

"No. Not on your own." He pressed his lips to her forehead, and she found herself briefly closing her eyes, finding that simple touch also seemed to leach away some of her stress. "I'm here to help. Starting with talking to your crew if they have questions."

"Thank you." Their eyes met, and the reassuring touch of his hands on her arms made her wish it were that easy. That poor John hadn't died, that she wasn't beyond shorthanded, that she wouldn't likely have to spend time away from the dig getting the Wagners settled back in Delphi or heading home, whichever they wanted. That anyone deciding to stay wouldn't be risking their health. That she wasn't facing imminent failure at what she'd wanted so much to accomplish. "They didn't say much. It might be good if you talked to them now. Maybe they'd feel more free to say or ask things with me out of the room."

"All right." He gave her arms a squeeze. "I don't have clinic appointments until nine. If—"

"Laurel! Laurel!"

They both turned to see Becka limping down the stairs, grabbing the handrail as she stumbled in her hasty descent. Panic was etched on her face, and an echo of it filled Laurel too, making her stomach clench. What could possibly be wrong now?

Andros leapt up a few steps to grasp Becka's arm. "Steady now, before you fall."

"Oh, thank God you're here, Dr. Drakoulias!" The girl clutched at him. "It's Jason. He's really sick. I think—" She gulped down a little sob. "I think he has what the Wagners have. And...and John. Oh, God, what are we going to do?"

CHAPTER TEN

LAUREL SAT IN the dirt on the side of the baking mountain, bagging and labeling potsherds, barely paying attention as she did. Wondering why she was even bothering.

It was over. Finished. She wasn't going to prove her parents' theory. She wasn't going to get their names in archaeological journals one last time, and her own too, to jump-start her belated, fledgling career. Probably wouldn't even receive the grant she'd wanted so badly, enabling her to get going on a project of her own. One that would inch her toward accomplishing at least an iota of what her parents had accomplished by her age.

How could they have died for nothing? Why couldn't their last excavation have been worth more than potsherds and jewelry and artifacts that, while interesting, were similar to all those already unearthed in Delphi?

She'd wanted that for them. For herself, and for

her sisters, giving them a small feeling of peace over her parents' passing. And now? Now she had to wonder if this work, their work, had been worth the very high cost.

Worth all the summers they'd had only a long-distance relationship with their girls. All the times Laurel had tried to play parent, while they had dug for history. Worth the hole left in their family that had started to form even before they'd died.

She swiped her dusty hands across her wet cheeks. John's family would be feeling the same emptiness, wondering why and for what, and her chest felt even heavier.

So often when digging, she could feel the spirits of the ancient people who'd lived there, hear them speaking, see them cooking in a vessel they'd unearthed, or wearing the jewelry they'd found. Sometimes it even felt as though the hand of fate was guiding her, showing her exactly where an artifact might be, drawing her there. But today the mountain was silent.

She pushed to her feet and looked into one of the wide, deep pits. The one that had been pains-takingly re-excavated after her parents had been crushed by its walls. Her throat got so tight she could barely squeeze out the words. "So this is it, Mom, Dad. This is the best I could do, and I know it's not nearly enough. Not what you would have expected of me. I'm sorry."

She gathered up the few bags, walked the worn goat path to her car and cleaned up before driving to the hospital in Vlychosia. Andros had arranged for Jason to be transported there, and, no matter how much it hurt, she owed the living more than she owed the dead. Starting with Jason, to see how he was and see if there was anything she could do to help. Then talking with Mel and Tom to tell them the dig was over. To ask what she could do for them as well.

She peeked into Mel and Tom's hospital room, surprised they weren't there, and a jolt of alarm went through her, sending her quickly back out of the room. Had they gotten worse? Were they back in the ICU?

Heart pounding, she practically ran down the hall, trying to find someone she could ask. She spotted two men in doctors' coats about to round a corner, one with thick dark hair, a sculpted jaw and a muscular frame, and knew without a doubt who it was. "Andros!"

He stopped and turned, spoke to the man with him, then moved in her direction. She jogged toward him, breathless. "Where are Mel and Tom? They're not worse, are they?"

"No, no. They're fine." He cupped her face in his warm palm for a moment before sliding it down to her shoulder. "In fact, they're being released. I was going to drive them back to the hotel after all the paperwork's done."

She took a deep breath of relief. "What about Jason?"

"Not sure yet, but so far not worse. He's getting good nursing care, so let's hope for the best." He looked at his watch. "How about a cup of coffee? They won't be ready to go for maybe another hour."

She didn't know if coffee would lift her spirits or jangle her nerves even more. Regardless, being with Andros would be the one thing sure to help her feel at least marginally better.

The coffee shop was surprisingly large, but the tables were tiny, their knees bumping against one another's beneath it. He reached for her hand, and his warm strength felt so comforting, she twined her fingers within his.

"You talked to the dig crew, right?" he asked.

"Yes. I told them to make their travel plans to go home."

"Good." His brows were pinched together in a small frown as his thumb absently stroked up and down hers. "We want them to wait a few days before getting on a plane. Or being close to other people. Quarantined, basically. And I also want blood tests from everyone. If no one else gets sick, you can all go."

"You did blood tests for the Wagners and John. You know it wasn't a fungal infection."

"We're looking at other possibilities. With John dead and three others sick, the national infection-control folks are involved. We'll be doing a battery of tests this time, a viral serology panel, looking for emerging infections. Something we maybe haven't seen before. Takes a long time to determine something that complicated, though, so I don't expect we'll know anything for a while yet."

His tone was as serious as his expression, and she realized it was a very good thing she'd shut down the dig. The pain she felt over not achieving her dream, her parents' dream, would be far worse if anyone else got sick. "It seems impossible that all this has something to do with the dig. But I know my parents wouldn't want anyone else to die trying to accomplish what they didn't have a chance to."

"Plenty's been achieved in the last five years of that dig, Laurel. Right? What more could there be to accomplish?"

She felt the supportive hold of his hand in hers, looked at the sincerity in his eyes, the caring, and nearly told him. But her lips closed and she shook her head. Even now, with the dig ending, she found she couldn't. Why, she wasn't sure, but it just seemed she should still keep the secret her parents had held close. "You never know. That's what makes you keep digging."

"I just realized I don't even know where you call home. I'd like to know, so when I think of you I can picture you there."

Home? Did she have such a thing anymore?

She'd been so consumed with everything that had happened, she hadn't even thought about leaving here in a few days. About not seeing him again. But the low, husky voice, the serious dark depths of his eyes, put that reality front and center. Added another layer of weight to her heart.

"Indiana. After my parents died, the only digs I worked on had to be close to where we lived, studying protohistoric Caborn-Welborn culture. But I recently sold the house, since my sisters don't need a place to roost anymore. And because I hope to head to Turkey soon, making that home for a while." If she could get the funding, which would be tough going, now. And why didn't that thought bother her as much as it had just last week? Must be the depressing reality of everything that had happened since.

"Protohistoric what?" His eyes crinkled at the corners, and just looking at his beautiful features caught her breath. "That's all Greek to me."

Trust him to somehow make her smile, and he did too, just before he leaned across the tiny table and kissed her. Long and slow and sweet, and when he pulled back, the eyes that met hers weren't smiling anymore.

"If you think this thing might be contagious and that some of us might have it, you shouldn't be kissing me, you know." She was trying to lighten the moment, but her chest felt even heavier, knowing it just might be their last kiss anyway.

"Too late. But even if it wasn't, it's worth the risk."

Worth the risk? Her heart fluttered, and she thought of the moonstones, and their teasing about them. Wished maybe she'd gotten them after all, to remember him by.

As though she needed anything to help her with that.

"Andros."

They looked up to see Dr. Galanos standing there. "The Wagners are ready to go. I've arranged for them and the whole crew to stay in quarantine here. Getting it ready now, and it should be comfortable enough. Which of you is going to get the Wagners' things from Delphi and bring back the rest of the dig crew?"

"I am." Laurel stood and, with a tightness squeezing her chest, braced herself for goodbye. "Thanks for all you've done for us, Andros."

"Your car won't fit everybody. I'll help drive the crew back here."

"Thank you." Only a couple more hours before

she didn't get to look at him anymore. Until they said goodbye one last time.

Their days in quarantine had seemed to drag on forever, and Laurel was glad it was finally over. Relieved that not a single team member had shown any symptoms at all. Beyond relieved that Jason had improved so much, they'd agreed to release him and let him go back to the States with them.

Andros had stopped in once, apparently meeting with Dr. Galanos. She and the Wagners had filled their time going through all the dig notes, writing summaries and outlines of the papers they'd publish, but it still hadn't been enough distraction for her to not hope it was Andros every time someone came in the room. For her to hope he'd stop in one more time to say goodbye.

But, really, why should he? It was a long drive from Kastorini, he'd likely been busy at the clinic, and it wasn't as though they were anything more than passing friends. Briefly lovers, though that fleeting moment was etched in her mind far more clearly than any other love affair she'd experienced.

She and the Wagners walked to the car to pack

it up before they left for the airport to go home. It struck her that the word *home* felt hollow, just as it had when Andros had asked where she'd lived. What was there for her, other than her short-term teaching-assistant position? Finishing up the final pieces to her PhD?

Somehow, she had to get that grant for the dig she'd been so enthusiastic about just months ago. The dig she knew her parents would have been proud she'd pursued. With any luck, she could find some success with that and push past this strangely restless emptiness in her chest.

"I feel like I've been in this hospital a month instead of nine days," Tom grumbled good-naturedly as he tossed their bags into the car.

"The best days of your life, considering we're still here on earth, thanks to the good care we got," Mel said.

"I know. And part of me feels odd, leaving. Like we should be going back to the dig to finish."

"Really?" Laurel stuffed her bag behind his and stared at him in surprise. "After the ordeal you've been through, I thought you'd run and never look back."

"They still don't know if it had any damn thing

to do with the dig. If I felt strong enough, I'd go back right now, but I know I'm not up to it," Tom said, stopping in the midst of packing Mel's bag to give Laurel a long look that struck her as very odd.

"What? Why are you looking at me like that?"

"I just…I'm not sure I should tell you, but, ah, hell." He grabbed the back of his neck and sighed. "You know how sometimes we all get that feeling on a dig, like an invisible finger is pointing and you just have to follow it and look?"

Her heart sped up a little. "Yes. I know."

"I felt it in the cave. That last day. Real strong and compelling. Leading me toward the far left wall, just past a huge orange stalactite, about a hundred feet back. Farther in than we'd been excavating. I was going to dig some, but it got late and I wasn't feeling too good. I figured I'd be able to tackle it better the next morning."

"Which all could have been delirium, since that was the night you got really sick," Mel said. She wore a deep frown, shaking her head slightly at him.

"You think that's where it might be," Laurel said, barely able to breathe.

"I do. Mel doesn't want you to go in there, but honestly? I really think we were close. My gut just tells me it might be there."

She looked from Tom to Mel and back again, a surge of adrenaline roaring through her blood. Without one more second of thought, she yanked her bag back out of the car and could practically feel her parents pushing her on the way they so often had, even when she'd been frustrated by it. Wanting her to use these final two weeks to search a little longer.

She'd learned to listen to little voices in her head, whoever or whatever they might be. And these little voices? They might be the most important whispers she would ever hear.

"I'm going back." She leaned in to kiss Mel on the cheek, then Tom. "I'll keep you posted."

"Laurel." Mel reached for her. "I know your parents expected a lot from you. Were driven, and drove you too. And you always stepped up, no matter how hard it was. But they wouldn't want you to risk getting sick. Risk your life. Let it go. You have other digs in your future."

"But not a dig like this one. And like Tom said, you getting sick might have had nothing to do with the dig anyway. But I'll be careful. I'll wear gloves and a mask. It'll be okay."

"I know there's no point in arguing with you when you've made up your mind." The woman who'd stepped in to do quite a bit of mothering after Laurel's parents were gone gave her a fierce hug. "Promise you'll be careful. Promise you'll stay safe."

"I will. I'll see you back at the university in two weeks, and with any luck there'll be a treasure in my pocket."

"A little too big for your pocket," Tom said, hugging her and grinning. "If you find it, they'll build a whole new room for it in the Delphi museum, with your parents' names on the plaque. So many visitors will flock to see it, the Charioteer will be damn jealous."

"We'll drive you back," Mel said.

"No, I'll rent another car. Don't worry about me. Adventure is what I live for, remember?"

Funny how the day seemed blindingly brighter. Her chest filled with an excitement and energy she hadn't felt since before the Wagners got sick. And that excitement and energy sent her thoughts to Andros. Bombarded with memories of how he made her feel exactly that way too.

By the time she got the car rented and arrived back in Delphi, there was too little daylight left to head up the mountain to the dig. Being back in town made her thoughts turn to Andros again. Of strolling through the streets, feeding the cats, kissing him until she was breathless. Walking into the hotel filled her with memories of kissing him again on the back deck and of making love with him in her slightly lumpy little bed.

Not that she hadn't thought of him more times than she could count the past three days and nights in Vlychosia anyway.

Maybe after she checked in, she should call him. Just to let him know she was back. Then again, she knew he'd be unhappy with her going back to the dig, and even more unhappy that her first stop would be the caves, which she hadn't been in even once. And that he still believed might be the source of the mysterious pneumonia.

She didn't need the man's approval or permission or lectures. She'd been on her own for a long time, so why did she feel this need, this longing, really, to get in touch with him?

No. She shook her head and grabbed up her duffel. She'd been given one more chance to find the treasure. Tonight she'd look at the map of the caves, carefully drawn over the past three years, read through all Tom's notes, and make a plan. A plan that didn't include making love with Andros Drakoulias again.

"Hello, Spiros," she said to the desk clerk. "I'm back. Can I have the same room, or do you need to move me?"

The young man looked over his shoulder twice, then finally focused on her. The expression on his face could only be described as alarmed, and she wondered if the media coverage and the quarantine had spooked everyone.

"I am sorry, miss, but there are no rooms left."

"I'm absolutely fine, Spiros. The hospital gave us all a clean bill of health." She fished in her purse for the papers they'd given her, holding them out. "See?"

"I am sorry," he repeated. "But we did not know you were returning. We have rented every room for the next two weeks. I will call other hotels in Delphi for you, yes?"

"Thank you." She dropped her bag to the floor.

Why hadn't she been smart enough to call as soon as she'd known she was coming back? Regardless, it didn't really matter. A place to stay was a place to stay, so long as she could easily get to the dig.

As the minutes ticked away and Spiros made one call after another, concern grew to alarm. She might not be able to understand a word he was saying, but the frown and worried look were plain. Finding a room wasn't happening.

"I am sorry, miss," he said yet again, looking remorseful. "It is high season, you understand. Every room is booked by tours and others. I am sorry."

"Thank you for trying. I appreciate it." So now what? She hauled her duffle over her shoulder again and went out the door and across the still-hot blacktop. There was only one solution she could think of. And how ridiculous that the solution sent happiness surging through her veins, sending her practically running to her car and jumping inside.

There was one person nearby who'd said he was there to help her any way he could. Was it her fault she needed a little more help from him now?

CHAPTER ELEVEN

"ONE MORE STORY, Daddy? Please?"

Andros slid the book from his daughter's hands, an easy accomplishment since her fingers had gone limp, her words slow and slurred. "Not tonight. If you sleep tight, I'm sure your little fairies will visit."

She smiled at the same time her eyes closed. He watched her roll to her side, pull her sheet up to her chest and fall straight to sleep. He tugged the sheet a little higher to tuck it beneath her little chin, wondering all over again how he could possibly be so blessed.

The stairs creaked as he made his way back to the living room, absently thinking he should see if he could find a way to quiet them. His handyman skills weren't up there with his doctoring skills, but surely he could figure something out.

Right now, though, there was something more important to figure out. He propped up his feet, put his laptop on his knees, and did another advanced internet search to look at various known pathogens, common and uncommon. Trying to read through it all, he found it hard to concentrate on the information. Damned difficult, in fact, because he just couldn't stop thinking of Laurel.

Di had told him the entire archaeological team had been cleared to leave quarantine, including Jason, thankfully. Probably they were all at the airport by now, maybe even already on a plane bound for the States. Leaving unanswered questions behind them, but he and Di and the virologists would eventually figure it out. Had to, because even though no one in Delphi, Kastorini or any other nearby town had come down with anything similar, they all wanted it to stay that way.

He closed his eyes and pictured Laurel's face. Her amazing blue eyes and pretty lips that sometimes smiled or cutely twisted when she was thinking. Lips that had kissed him until he couldn't think straight. He pictured her slim figure and how sexy her rear looked in anything she wore, even those loose, dirty work shorts of hers with pockets everywhere. But his favorite had been that silky long dress. No, not quite. His favorite was how she'd looked when her hair had been released from its ponytail, spilling across the pillow and her soft skin, tangling in his fingers as he made love with her.

Damn. Just thinking about her, all of her, made his breath feel a little short and his heart feel a little empty. How was it possible he could miss a woman so much, when he'd barely spent more than a few days with her?

He'd itched to go to Vlychosia to see her, to say goodbye one last time. Nearly had gotten in his car more than once, but stopped himself. Last thing he'd want to do would be to hurt Laurel, which he hadn't even realized he'd done to some of the women who'd briefly been in his life. He wasn't made for a real relationship anyway, and, even if he had been, what was the point of getting too attached to a woman focused on spending her life at digs around the world? Or for Cassie to? A little girl who had lost her mother far too soon just might be unconsciously looking for someone to take her place.

No, it was good Laurel had moved on, leaving

no possibility of anyone getting hurt, or the storm of gossip he wanted to avoid.

He tried to refocus on the internet journal and the various viral beta groups, and was startled when his cell phone rang. He hoped it wasn't an emergency, but if he had to bundle up Cassie and take her the few houses down to his sister's, he suspected his little girl wouldn't lift an eyelid.

He dug his phone from his pocket. His heart jerked hard and his breath caught in his chest. Laurel. What could she be calling about?

"Dr. Drakoulias." He'd answered that way to keep his voice sounding calm and professional. Unemotional, so she wouldn't know how much he'd been thinking of her. Missing her.

"Is this the Dr. Drakoulias who told me he was here to help if I needed it? Unfortunately, I have a little problem."

"That would be me." Her voice sounded normal, with even that touch of humor he liked so much, so there must not be some terrible problem. He relaxed at the same time he felt instantly wired, alert, elated too, because hearing her on the other end of the line was like being given an unexpected gift. "What is this little problem?"

"Well, believe it or not, I'm in Delphi. But the hotel gave my room away, and there's not another room to be had in the entire town."

"You're in Delphi?"

"Yep, I am."

"And you need a place to stay." He couldn't imagine why she'd come back, but the way his heart had jerked in his chest when she'd first called was nothing to the gymnastics it was doing now.

"I'm afraid I do. There are a few hotels in Kastorini, aren't there?"

"One's full up for a wedding this weekend, which I know because a patient talked to me about it for half an hour today. The other two usually take on overflow from Delphi, so I bet they're booked too."

"That's what Spiros at my hotel told me." She sighed in his ear. "Is there any way I can hole up in the clinic or something, just for one night while I check out nearby towns tomorrow? Or maybe even briefly stay with Taryn?"

"My house has three bedrooms. No reason to call Taryn tonight, you can just stay here." The instant the words were out of his mouth, he pictured her here with him, sitting in his cozy living room, fascinating him with stories about the dig and about her life. Tousled and sleepy when he fixed her coffee in the morning. He wondered what she wore to bed, and a vision of something silky and skimpy came to mind, or, even better, her completely naked, glorious body. But even if she slept in an oversized T-shirt, she'd look sexy as hell.

That vision faded when he realized if anyone found out he had a woman staying in his house, the tongues would flap like crazy. And what were the odds no one would know? Pretty much zero out of a hundred. But he couldn't worry about that when Laurel needed someplace to lay her head. "Cassie's in bed, but she sleeps like a rock. Won't even blink if I put her in the car to come get you."

"Thank you." Her voice got softer, warmer. "But I rented another car. I'll be there in about twenty minutes, if that's okay."

"I'll be waiting." And each minute of it would seem like two. At the moment, there was no way he'd get one thing out of the clinical information on his laptop, and he closed it, realizing the house could use some spiffing up. Cassie's toys lying all around didn't bother him, but probably making sure Laurel didn't turn an ankle stepping on one would be a good idea.

His arms were full of the last of it—multicolored plastic blocks he was trying to find the box to dump into—when there was a soft knock on the door. It opened a few inches, and beautiful blue eyes met his through the crack. "Hi. It's me. Didn't want to wake Cassie by ringing the doorbell."

"Nothing wakes that child up. Come on in."

The sight of all of her, not just those amazing eyes, caught his breath. She was wearing that dress he loved so much that embraced every curve, and her hair—God, her hair was down, out of her usual ponytail, falling in a shimmering golden waterfall over her shoulders. He stood there staring like a fool, an armload of plastic stuff preventing him from pulling her into his arms and kissing her until she was as breathless as he felt.

But maybe she didn't want that. Yes, they'd made love after the stress of learning about John's failing health, but that didn't mean she wanted to go there again. And he wanted her to feel comfortable in his house, not worried he might jump on her any moment like a flea on a kitten.

On the other hand, he might not be imagining the way she was looking at him. A way that said she might not mind him jumping on her at all.

Where was that damned box? "You don't happen to see a white box with pictures of blocks on it, do you?"

"Is this it?" She walked to the small door under the stairs where they stored Cassie's stuff. He'd already stuck a few things in there, and she bent over to open the door wider. He got so fixated on her shapely rear in that dress, he hardly noticed she was pulling the elusive box out from behind a huge stuffed lion.

"How come I put things in there twice and didn't see it?"

"I'm good at excavating, remember?" She held out the box, and he dumped the blocks inside. She turned and bent over again to shove the thing back behind the lion, and Andros gave up trying to keep his distance.

"You do realize you bending over in that sexy dress of yours is testing the limits of my gentlemanliness?"

"Is it?" She turned to him and took a step toward him, the amusement in her eyes mingling with the same heat he was trying to bank down. "Funny. Just looking at you in your T-shirt and jeans with your hair a little messy makes me want to test it even further."

To his shock and delight, she closed the gap between them, tunneled her hands into his hair and kissed him.

He wrapped his arms around her, lost in the taste of her, the intoxicating flavor he'd thought he'd never get to taste again. Her silky hair slid over his hands, his forearms, as he pressed her even closer, loving the feel of her every soft curve pressed against his body.

Still clutching his head, she broke the kiss and stared into his eyes. "I kept hoping you'd come back to the hospital one more time. To say goodbye."

"So you came to say goodbye?" He'd thought she'd already gone. So why did the thought of a goodbye now feel so bad?

"Not yet. Right now I'm saying hello."

"I like hellos better than goodbyes," he murmured against her lips before he kissed her again.

The way she melted against him, gasping softly into his mouth as their tongues leisurely danced, made him think maybe she'd missed him too. That maybe she'd thought of him as much as he had her the past few days.

But she had a life in the States and a PhD to finish and papers to write. Grants to get and new digs to work on. Thinking of him or not, why had she come back?

"How long are you in town? And why?"

She drew back a few inches. "Well, I have some unfinished business. Don't know how long it might take, but—"

The shrill ring of his phone interrupted, and he nearly cursed it. He hated letting go of Laurel's warm body, but it would seem pretty odd to dance her over to the side table to answer the damn thing. "Dr. Drakoulias."

"Andros! It's Yanni. Dora's having the baby. Thinks it's coming soon."

"Do you think she's able to get to the clinic?"

"Yes. I think so."

"I'll meet you there." *Damn.* Timing being what it always was, Christina was in Athens for a few days. Not to mention that things just might have been leading somewhere very good with Laurel. "I'm sorry. Got to go deliver a baby that apparently is in a hurry to get here. Excuse me again."

He dialed the nurse midwife in Levadia who was on call for Christina. He huffed out an impatient breath when her husband said she'd gone to the grocery store. Didn't on call mean on call? "I need to hear from her as soon as possible."

"What's wrong?" Laurel asked. "You worried about the mother?"

"No. She's had a healthy pregnancy. But this is her fifth, and if she thinks it's coming soon, I believe her. Christina's not here, and the midwife on call isn't home. And it'll take her half an hour to get here anyway."

"Let me help. I mean, you just need an assistant, right? I don't need to be a nurse or anything?"

"Just need an assistant. Are you sure you're up for that?"

"Sounds like it would be an experience, and, hey, I'm always up for an adventure."

"Never thought of bringing a baby into the world as an adventure, but I guess it can be." He'd already seen the woman didn't back down from a challenge and had to smile. "It'll be faster if Taryn brings Petros here. I'll call her, then we can go."

"Looks like they're not here yet, which is good," Andros said as he pulled the car up to the clinic. "You can help me get stuff set up."

Nervous but excited too, Laurel followed Andros back to the hospital wing. She couldn't believe she was about to see a baby being born, maybe even be a part of bringing it into the world. Hadn't thought she'd ever want to, but, now that it was about to happen, she knew it would probably be an amazing experience.

Andros wheeled over a small cart from a corner with what looked like maybe a heating unit above it, and put a tiny little oxygen mask in the corner of the little crib, hooking it up to something. He pulled other strange things out from the supply cupboard, laid them on a thick metal table next to the hospital bed, then grabbed more items in his arms.

"I don't want to get in the way, but is there anything I can do?"

"I'm good right now, thanks." He tossed her a couple of plastic bags with what looked like blue paper inside. "Can you go see if Yanni and Dora are outside and bring them in here? Then put on that gown. Gloves too, after you come back, because I'll need you to handle the baby."

Handle the baby? What if she dropped it on its head or something? Nerves jabbed into her belly at the thought, though she should have realized she might have to take care of the newborn while he took care of the mother.

As soon as she got to the front door, a car zoomed up the street and swerved in front of the clinic, parking crooked. She rushed out of the door, hoping like heck the woman wasn't already spitting out the baby right there in the car, but if she had to catch the newborn, then, darn it, she would. A man leaped out and practically flew around to the passenger door, looking a little wild-eyed.

"Do you need help? Dr. Drakoulias is inside—do you want me to get him?"

"*Ochi*. I can bring her."

He swung the woman into his arms, and she wrapped her hands around his neck before burying her face in his chest. Her distressed cry was muffled, but Laurel's gut tightened, hearing her sound of pain. She ran to hold open the door and led the way to the clinic.

"Follow me."

Andros had already changed into scrubs and was busy putting towels next to the bed. He looked up and smiled. "Always in a hurry, Dora. Ever since we were in grade school."

The woman looked up and gave him a wavering smile back. She spoke in Greek so Laurel didn't know what she'd said in return, but apparently the woman still managed to have a sense of humor despite everything, as both men laughed.

Then just that fast, she apparently had another contraction, crying out as her face contorted. All humor was replaced by worry on her husband's face as he laid her on the bed, speaking to her soothingly. The sweetness and caring in his eyes tugged at Laurel's heart, and she wished she'd talked to her parents about what it had been like the times their own brood had been born. Made her wonder, for the first time, why they'd even had four children when their careers had been such a huge priority. Had their family been more important to them than she'd realized?

"I'm going to speak English, as Laurel doesn't

speak Greek," Andros said, "so she understands what she needs to do to help. Okay?"

Both nodded, and he turned to Laurel. "Help me get her clothes off and a gown on her, please." Despite the strangeness of the situation, it felt oddly normal to work together with him, and they quickly had Dora ready. Laurel was surprised it didn't also seem uncomfortable for the lower half of the woman to be completely naked, but maybe since it was obviously the last thing the woman was concerned about, it seemed like no big deal.

"This is an external probe, to monitor the baby's heartbeat." Andros attached a belt to her swollen belly, with some electronic gadget attached to it. "It's not as accurate as an internal probe we sometimes attach to a baby's head, but since your little one wants to come soon, I think this is good, okay?"

Both nodded again, obviously having complete faith in Andros, and Laurel looked at his face. Calm, but completely in command, and she knew she'd have the same exact confidence in him no matter what the situation.

"Are you all right? Do you want pain relief, Dora?"

"*Ochi.* No time. The baby…is coming."

He glanced at the monitor and his expression was neutral, but it seemed to Laurel it tensed a bit. "Baby's heart rate is dropping a little, Dora. Called bradycardia. Could be just from contractions, but we need to keep an eye on it."

"What do you mean?"

"If there's sustained fetal bradycardia, we'll need to get the baby out as fast as possible. Not to worry, though. And see? It's already recovering a bit."

Dora gave a sudden, extended cry, so agonized, Laurel winced for her. Yanni gripped her hand, looking nearly as distressed as his wife did. Laurel was so focused on the poor woman's pain she didn't notice Andros was leaning over the woman.

"You weren't kidding about it coming soon, Dora! Baby's on the way. The head is crowning. Time to push."

Laurel stared in amazement when she saw the top of the baby's head begin to emerge. She'd wondered if it might be gross or icky to see, but it wasn't at all. It was awe inspiring. Incredible.

"Oh, my gosh, it's right there!" She hadn't meant to exclaim that out loud and looked guiltily at

Andros. He kept his attention on the baby and mother, but that surprise dimple poked into his cheek and she knew he was smiling.

"Yes. He or she will be here soon. Push again, Dora."

The woman grunted and groaned and pushed as her husband murmured encouragingly to her, but the baby didn't seem to move.

"Baby's heart rate is dropping again, Dora. We need to get the baby out. Laurel, I need you to put fundal pressure on top of the uterus."

"Fundal pressure?" Laurel's heart beat harder. She hoped she was up to whatever task this was he needed her to do.

"Basically, I need you to put your hands on the top of her belly and push hard. Put your weight into it."

"Um, okay." She positioned herself next to the woman and spread her hands on Dora's belly, feeling a little weird and a lot nervous. She pushed down, worried she might hurt her. "Like this?"

"Harder. As hard as you can."

Holy crap. "I'm afraid I'll hurt her."

"You won't. And we need to get the baby out."

Andros's intense expression sent her heart

pumping even harder, and she gritted her teeth and put everything she could into pushing on the surprisingly hard expanse of poor Dora's belly. In the midst of the woman panting and pushing, and her husband speaking tensely in words that were probably supposed to be encouraging, Andros suddenly said, sharply, "Stop, Laurel. Stop pushing, Dora."

"What? Why?" Dora gasped.

"Baby's heartbeat is dropping again because the cord is around its neck. Give me a minute."

Almost as short of breath as the laboring mother, Laurel stared down at the baby's head, now out of its mother's body and being held gently in Andros's hands. Then her breath stopped completely and she felt a little woozy when she saw the baby was beyond blue, and the umbilical cord was wrapped several times around its neck.

She sucked in quick breaths to calm herself. Big help she'd be if she fainted in the middle of the birth. Andros slid his fingers carefully beneath the cord, gently loosening and unwrapping it, then finally slipping it completely off over the baby's head. "Okay, ready now. Let's have a last few good pushes, Dora. You're doing great. Can you help her, Laurel?"

Fear gave Laurel super energy, and she pushed hard on Dora's belly as the woman worked to deliver her child. After a few monumental pushes, the baby slipped from its mother's body into the waiting hands of Dr. Andros Drakoulias.

"Another girl!" Andros said, glancing up with a smile so big that that dimple of his showed again. "And she's as beautiful as her mother."

Dora sagged back, gasping and beaming, looking from the baby to her husband and back again. Yanni leaned forward to give her a lingering kiss, speaking soft words in her ear that Laurel couldn't understand, but at the same time she knew exactly what he must be saying.

Laurel felt about as wrung out as Dora, but wired too. She watched Andros rub the baby gently all over with a towel then put a bulb into her mouth to suction out fluids. The tiny thing seemed alarmingly blue, and the seconds seemed like minutes before the baby's head finally began to pink up, then her torso, as she cried out in lusty breaths.

The parents laughed and kissed, Andros grinned, and Laurel sagged, letting out a huge sigh of relief.

What an amazing experience. Scary and exhilarating and wonderful and unforgettable.

"You did a great job, Dora. Baby's had a bit of a rough time, so we need to get her warmed up and breathing well before I hand her over to mama." Andros's gaze met Laurel's. "Are you okay handling the baby, Laurel? She needs to be dried off with the towels to warm her up, wrapped with a dry one, then put under the heat lamp and given oxygen. I already have it turned on, so just position the mask over her mouth. I need to take care of Dora."

"Yes. Of course." She hurried over, not knowing exactly what to do, but whatever it was, she knew Andros would guide her through it if she messed up somehow.

He handed her the still slightly wet baby, and a moment of terror nearly stopped her heart. What if she dropped it?

"Don't worry. She's not glass." Andros gave her an encouraging smile. "Just dry her off like you would a little puppy after its bath, swaddle her up, then put her in the warmer." Andros grinned as though he'd read her mind, and she wondered what expression was on her face for him to see.

Heart thumping, she grabbed up a towel and carried the baby to the warmer. Softly, she began stroking the child with the towel, dumbstruck at the little brown eyes staring up at her as she did. As though the baby, just a few minutes old, was avidly studying her brand-new world.

"Dora, I'm going to give you some oxytocin to help your uterus clamp down and stop the bleeding. Okay?"

Laurel didn't look behind her, but knew the new mother wore the same expression on her face she'd had all along. Complete confidence that Andros would take care of everything.

She finished drying the baby, marveling at her mini fingers and feet, her tiny elbows and knees, then awkwardly swaddled her, sure any nurse would laugh at the pitiful job. The immeasurable good Andros accomplished every day struck her with awe. Yes, she loved her job. Following in her parents' footsteps. Uncovering history, learning from the past, was valuable to humankind's education. But this?

This put it in perspective. A dig wasn't life or

death. It was about past lives and past deaths, but, when it came right down to it, helping others today and now was the most important thing anyone could do.

Helping her sisters become the people they'd become had been more important than getting her PhD done. More important than any dig, no matter how meaningful. She was glad to be free of the responsibility now, but postponing those things to raise and guide her sisters had been the biggest accomplishment of her life so far. How had she never appreciated that before?

The little baby staring at her from under the heat lamp raised her downy eyebrows, seeming to agree. Laurel smiled, stroking the infant's soft cheek, feeling a strangely serene, inner calm she couldn't remember feeling since before her parents died. For the first time, she realized that maybe having a baby of her own one day had its place on her list of life goals.

She'd head back to the mountain, into the caves, tomorrow. Hopefully she'd bring to a close her number-one goal. She'd leave no stone unturned to make it happen. But if she didn't?

She'd remember this sweet little baby's face, and be at peace with the outcome, knowing she'd given it everything she could.

CHAPTER TWELVE

"DID YOU REALLY help Daddy born a baby, Laurel?" Cassie asked as the three of them sat at the breakfast table, her usual excitement on her adorable face and sparkling in her brown eyes.

"I did. It was amazing. Your daddy's pretty amazing too." She looked at him over her coffee cup, struck all over again by his astonishing physical beauty, somehow magnified even more by the dark stubble on his chin and the faded T-shirt stretching across his thick chest and arms. And his inner beauty too, which she'd seen last night. Radiating competence and caring, reassuring the mother throughout even the scariest part of the birth.

"I know," Cassie said as she stuffed a piece of bread into her mouth. "How did I look when I was born, Daddy? Did I cry a lot?"

Andros stilled in midmotion, his gaze meeting Laurel's before he put his cup back down.

"I wasn't there when you were born, remember, sweetie?"

Laurel's chest squeezed at his somber expression. Obviously, this was a painful subject for him, and she wondered when she'd finally find out about his relationship with Cassie's mother and how she'd died. A woman he'd said he wasn't close to. The knowledge that Cassie didn't have a mother made her heart ache for the child. But she was lucky to have a father who so obviously loved her, and an extended family too, in Taryn and Petros and her grandparents. Laurel knew from experience that could make even a terrible loss more bearable.

"Oh. I forgot." Cassie went back to eating, not seeming very bothered by the conversation, which eased the tightness in Laurel's chest. "When are we going fishing, Daddy?"

"As soon as you're done eating. I want to see that apricot go down the hatch." He picked it up and held it to her mouth and she lunged at it, nearly biting his fingers. "Ouch! Are you a wild dog this morning? I need all my fingers, you know."

Cassie giggled. "I'm a monster fairy. I have tiny teeth, but they're very sharp and hurty."

"Monster fairy? Sounds like a compromise with Petros."

His amused eyes met Laurel's, and they smiled together in an oddly intimate connection. How could sitting here at their breakfast table feel so normal, so right, when she didn't really know either of them all that well? How could it remind her of her own family, of breakfasts with her parents and her sisters that were the best memories of her life?

Moments she'd taken completely for granted until they were in the past. Until they could never happen again.

"You're not working today, Andros?" she asked, wondering how the only doctor in town had time to fish.

"Since Christina's gone a few days, I closed the clinic. Off work to play with Cassie, unless there's an emergency."

"Are you coming fishing with us, Laurel?"

"I can't. Unlike your dad, I don't have the day off." Filled with a sudden longing to join them, she fought it back. She hadn't been given this one last chance to find the treasure just to twiddle away the little time she had. Andros's brows quirked at her in a questioning look and she braced herself. The man would not be happy about her plans to go in the cave, but it wasn't his decision. Wasn't his parents' dream she had one more shot at realizing. Her chance to make them proud.

"With all the excitement, you never did tell me why you came back. What is it you still need to do?"

She opened her mouth to tell him then closed it again. Coward that she was, she didn't want to ruin this warm, pleasant moment they were sharing. And didn't she deserve just a few hours of relaxation and fun on the boat with them? Just for a little while before work took 100 percent of her time? The way it had for her parents?

"You know, work can wait a little while longer. Because, you might not believe this, but..." She leaned closer to Cassie. "I've never been fishing. Will you teach me how?"

"Yes! I will! Can I get my tackle box now, Daddy? Please?"

"All right. I'll pack up the last of your fruit for a snack."

Laurel smiled as the child leaped from the chair and ran off, her spindly little legs practically a blur. Maybe it made her nosy, but she couldn't help being curious about Cassie's mother and what Andros had said before. Now might be the only chance she had to ask without the little girl around.

"So. Maybe enjoying a little nakedness together doesn't give me the right to ask," she began, wondering why she felt suddenly nervous, like maybe she didn't want to know the answer after all, "but Cassie is the sweetest little thing, and I can't help but wonder about her mom. You said she passed away?"

Andros stared down into his coffee cup, not responding, exactly the way he'd acted when she'd brought the subject up on the mountain. That seemed like a long time ago now, but just as she was about to apologize for asking, for butting into something that wasn't her business, he looked up and fully met her gaze.

"Yes. As I said before, it's a sad thing for Cassie. But the rest of the story? It isn't one I'm particularly proud of."

Oh, Lord. Probably this really was something she didn't want to know and she wished she'd kept her mouth shut at the same time that she found herself desperately needing to hear it.

"I spent my youth going from one girlfriend to the next. Thought that was a good thing, what guys did, right? Now I wish my parents had yanked me aside and lectured me on respecting women, but they didn't. Don't know if they turned a blind eye or honestly weren't aware of it until after I left and they heard the gossip, but by the time I left Kastorini for school in the States, I had quite a reputation."

"You're a beautiful man, Andros, which I'm sure you know." Hadn't she about swooned the very first time she'd set eyes on him? "I bet it was a two-way street, with girls throwing themselves at you."

"Doesn't mean you have to take advantage of it. But I did. And when I saw the big, wide world of a college campus, then med school and residency? I felt like I'd moved from dinner to a full banquet."

"And you feel guilty about that." She could see it in his eyes. Guilt. And while a part of her felt uncomfortable, maybe even a little cheap at being just another woman who'd offered herself up at that banquet, she also believed he was no longer that young, careless man.

"Yes. I do." His eyes met hers again, intense and sincere. "Even before I found out about Cassie, I'd started to grow up. To see that women weren't something to be enjoyed at random, even if that seemed to be all they wanted, too. I took a step back to think about who I was and who I wanted to be. Figured I just wasn't capable of a lasting relationship with a woman. Had never wanted one, but knew I needed to start being more careful about who I got involved with so no one got hurt. Then I got a phone call that brought that lesson home for good."

Laurel knew what that phone call must have been. Her heart twisted in a knot, and she covered his hand with hers and waited.

"Alison's brother—Alison was Cassie's mother—called me. Said she'd died in a car accident, and I was listed on Cassie's birth certificate as the father. Her parents were older and couldn't take care of a toddler, and the brother was single and traveled a lot. So they decided to contact me."

This time, his dark eyes were filled with pain.

Remorse too, and her heart clutched even harder. "You didn't know."

"No. I didn't know. I wish she'd told me, though I hate to admit I barely remembered who she was. Maybe she didn't because she figured I'd be irresponsible."

"No, Andros, she had to know the caring man you are would have stepped up."

"Maybe, maybe not. When I first found out, there were plenty who knew me that doubted I would. And I wasn't sure I could blame them." He held her hand between both of his, his gaze not wavering from hers. "Maybe it happened later than it should have, but learning about Cassie brought me to that final step of realizing I was a man now, not a careless, self-absorbed boy. Which meant coming back to Kastorini to work with my father, as he'd always wanted me to. To raise Cassie here the way I'd been raised, to finally embrace the roots I'd been blessed to be given."

She tightened her hold on his hand, giving him a smile that she hoped showed she understood. That everyone had years they'd spent doing a whole lot of growing up, and it wasn't always tidy or pretty. Hadn't she struggled to guide her sisters, often failing miserably because of her own immaturity? "Gotta admit, I find it hard to believe there was a time you weren't sure you wanted to come back. I love it here. Your place—your town—is truly special." She had to bite back her next words, which had almost been *and you're every bit as special, too.*

"It is. Special, and hard for me to believe." A small smile played about his lips now, and she was glad to see it. Happy he'd felt able to share all that with her, and happy he saw she understood.

"By the way." He leaned in, a breath away. "Just so you know, you're not just another fling to me. You're damned special too."

Her heart knocked at the words she'd almost said to him. She saw his smile, slightly crooked and more than sexy, just before his mouth touched hers. Her eyes drifted closed to savor the sensation. Sweet and slow, tasting a little like coffee and a lot like warmth and pleasure and simple happiness. Just as she was sinking deep into all of it, a banged-open door, followed by a voice so loud it was hard to believe it came from a tiny little throat, interrupted.

"Got everything, Daddy and Laurel! Let's go feed the fishies!"

* * *

Laurel would never have believed that such a soft, comfy cocoon of a bed would have left her tossing around with not nearly enough hours of sleep.

She'd sunk deep into its comfort, enjoying reliving the beautiful day she'd spent on the water with Cassie and Andros. Smiling as she remembered the tangled fishing lines and the hook that had flown back to snag her hair when Cassie had yanked too hard at an invisible fish she'd been sure was on the line. Seeing Andros's immediate concern when he'd jumped up to carefully extricate it, the expanse of his wide chest in front of her face for a temptingly long time, making it nearly impossible to not breathe him in. To not wrap her arms around as much of him as she could and kiss him senseless.

Thank heavens Cassie had been chaperone, or she knew she couldn't possibly have resisted. And that realization knocked away all those pleasant feelings, leaving her frowning at the ceiling. Wondering about this deep contentment she felt here, and worried about it too. She had to be happy and content when she moved on from here, and each hour she stayed made her realize it might be a bigger adjustment than she'd expected to become a rolling stone, living in various places around the world as she built her career.

The only thing that had marred the day slightly were reporters showing up to sniff around. Apparently a few locals knew she'd returned and told them she was on Andros's boat. That situation had him looking beyond grim, which seemed a little unnecessary. Though she supposed having to answer questions and calm worried locals was a stress he didn't need.

She caught herself drifting back to the lovely memories of the day on the boat and opened her eyes again, annoyed with herself. She'd come back to Kastorini to find the statue, not play around with and lust after Andros Drakoulias. Really, she hadn't meant to come to Kastorini at all, and if she'd been able to get her room back wouldn't even have seen him again.

Except she had to face that this stern self-lecture was partly a lie. Consciously or unconsciously, she knew she'd have looked for a reason to come back here, even if that reason had been something lame and inane.

She flopped to her side, pinching her eyelids closed, willing herself to sleep. Tomorrow had to be cave day. Not an easy day, either, since she hadn't worked in there at all and had only Tom's map and his "feeling" to help her find that statue. "And finding it means everything, remember?" she whispered fiercely to herself. "Everything."

Everything. Everything her parents had expected her to work toward. What her parents had died for. What was wrong with her that it seemed harder and harder to keep that at the forefront of her mind?

Her bleariness faded at breakfast, with Cassie's steady, cute chatter and two cups of coffee managing to help her feel upbeat again.

"A little more coffee, Laurel? Or more fruit?" Andros asked, holding up the pot.

"No, thank you, but it was delicious. If you'll excuse me, I have some things I need to get done today." She shoved herself from her chair and left the kitchen, feeling Andros's gaze on her back. What were the odds he wouldn't ask her what she was going to do, when she came down with her pack?

She didn't have to wonder long, as he stood just

a few feet away from the bottom of the stairs. Her trot down the steps slowed, and she braced herself.

"You can't be serious. Are you nuts?"

Andros stared at her with disbelief and anger etched all too clearly on his face. He folded his arms across his chest and took a step closer, as though his size and maleness would somehow intimidate her.

"What do you mean?"

"I'm not stupid, Laurel. You're obviously planning to go into the caves."

She took a step toward him and stared him down. Well, up, actually, since she was now only inches away from him.

"I know you don't understand. I don't expect you to. I'll wear a mask and gloves, just in case. But I need to look just a little longer."

"Look for what? More potsherds or a long-lost gold ring like countless others in Greek museums? Bones from thousands of years ago? I've talked to the Wagners about this dig, about the hundreds of items excavated. You've done plenty. Why can't you let it go? It's over."

"Not quite yet."

He turned to pace away a few steps, staring out

of the window. His posture was stiff, and frustration practically radiated from him. Her throat tightened and her conscience tugged at her heart. The man wasn't worried about a contagion infecting Delphi or Kastorini or anywhere else.

He was upset because he was worried about her. She couldn't stand to let him think she was just an idiot. A stubborn fool. She owed him the whole truth.

"Andros," she said softly, walking toward him to place her hand on his back. He didn't turn, didn't respond, and she inched closer until her body nearly touched his. "This isn't about a few more potsherds. There's something important my parents believed would be found at this site. Something that will rock the archaeological world. Something I want to find for them, and for myself."

He turned to look down at her, that deep frown still between his dark brows. The worry still there too, but not the anger. "What? What could be so important?"

"There's a lengthy poem inscribed on one of the stones excavated near Delphi. A poem that talks about the Pythian games and the Charioteer and a golden Artemis, Apollo's sister. After studying the interesting metaphors in this poem, Mom and Dad became convinced the golden Artemis really existed in the form of a statue."

"They've been excavating for five years here with no statue showing up, Laurel."

"I know. But…" She wrapped her fingers around the warm skin of his arms. "The Wagners always suspected it might have been hidden in the caves, to protect it from looters after people no longer worshipped at Delphi. Tom thinks he felt where it is. So I'm going to look there a few more times."

"Felt where it is? What the hell does that mean?"

"Sounds ridiculous, I know. But surely you've had moments where you just had a gut feeling about something? A diagnosis, maybe, that comes to mind and seems right?"

He looked at her, not answering. After a long, tense moment, he finally shook his head and sighed. "You may be crazy, but even you know you can't go into a cave solo. I'll go with you."

"Andros, you don't have to—"

"Yeah, I do." He pulled her against him, and the lips that touched her forehead were gentle, not at all angry, and she was so relieved, she found herself leaning against him. Slid her hands up to his strong shoulders as his mouth lowered to hers in a kiss filled with frustration and sweetness and a slowly building heat that curled her toes and sent her fingers tangling with his thick, silky hair.

The heavy-lidded eyes staring at her were utterly coal black as he pulled back and ran his thumb across her lower lip. The sensual touch sent her breathing even more haywire, and she nearly drew his thumb into her mouth. Until she quickly reminded herself that heading to the cave was her priority for the day, not having delicious, sweaty sex with the hunkiest doctor alive.

"I really appreciate you…coming with me. I'm ready to go when you are."

His gaze lingered on hers a moment longer before he wordlessly turned and headed upstairs.

CHAPTER THIRTEEN

"I WAS EXPECTING it to be wetter in here. But most of the moisture's on the stalactites and stalagmites, not the ground at all," Laurel said as they moved through the cave, the light from their lanterns and helmet lamps swinging in wide arcs on the low ceiling, rocky walls, and floor.

"There is ground water in some caves on the mountain. Wouldn't that destroy artifacts?"

"Depends on the artifact." She pulled out Tom's map and looked at it again, trying to orient herself. "I thought working in here would be better than the hot mountainside, but it's a little creepy, don't you think?"

"The big bad adventure woman thinks it's a little creepy?"

The amusement in his voice was loud and clear even through the mask he wore, and she gave his arm a playful swat. "You're telling me you like it in here?"

"Interesting formations around. But I frankly can't see how the hell you think you'll find anything. A statue like you're talking about couldn't be buried in solid rock. If it was here, surely it would have been found by now."

She wouldn't admit she'd been thinking exactly the same thing. But Tom knew a lot more than she did, and he thought it was still possible. Who was she to doubt, when they'd been inside for barely half an hour?

"He said he got his feeling when he was about a hundred feet in, on the left-hand side. Behind some orange stalactite." She held up her lantern, peering for something orange, so focused she stumbled over a small, mounded stalagmite and might have fallen if Andros's strong hand hadn't shot out to grab her arm.

"Steady, adventure girl. We're not in a big hurry, here."

"Easy for you to say. You're not the one who has to head back to the university before the start of the new term." The words sent an unexpected jab right into her solar plexus at the thought of never being here again. On this amazing mountain, or in beautifully charming Kastorini.

Of never seeing Andros and little Cassie again.

But that was the nature of the life she wanted, wasn't it? That she'd trained for. Spend months of the year somewhere, meet new and interesting people, then move on. Maybe get to see them again the following year if a dig continued. But getting attached to one place for too long? Not a good idea for an archaeologist.

Remembering that wasn't going to be easy.

Andros hadn't said a word in response, and she wondered if he was thinking what she was. That he'd miss her. That he wished they'd had a little more time together to light up, then burn out, this…thing that had formed between them.

Definitely hadn't had enough time for either. And of all her regrets, she knew that was the biggest.

So aware of his warm hand still holding her arm, she moved farther into the cave, then stopped dead. "Look! A huge orange stalactite, over there!" She pointed, looking up at Andros, and his eyes met hers above the mask, strangely dark and intense at the same time they were touched with the humor she loved to see there.

"If we find it, can we keep the discovery to our-selves so I can put it in my living room?"

"Wouldn't suit your homey decor too well, I don't think. Let's look."

The sound of his chuckle vibrated practically in her ear as he squeezed in next to her behind the stalactite, his chest touching her back in the narrow space. Her heart thumped as she scanned the area. At first it looked as if it was nestled in by more expanse of solid rock that ended in a tri-angular corner, covered by a thin, shimmering layer of crystal. The excitement that had bub-bled up in her chest when she'd first spotted the orange formation deflated a little as she moved in close to what she could now see was obviously a dead end.

"Looks like it stops right here," she said. "I won-der if Tom could have meant a different stalac-tite?"

"Maybe. Or his psychic feelings were really just indigestion." Andros wrapped his arm around her, splaying his gloved hand across her belly in a squeeze. A shiver slipped across her neck and down her spine as his deep voice murmured in her ear, "Gotta say, though, this cave is starting

2

43

to grow on me. I like being smashed into close quarters with you. Except it's hard to nuzzle your ear with this damn mask on."

"You're the one who insisted on the masks." She turned her face and their noses and mouths touched through the paper, making them both laugh a little breathlessly.

"Kissing you this way is still better than kissing anybody else's lips." The eyes that stared into hers were hot and amused and held an absurd sincerity that had her pressing her mask-covered mouth to his again.

"You're ridiculous," she said, forcing herself to turn back to the crevice and remember why the heck they were in this cave to begin with.

He held his lantern up above her head. "Or maybe it wasn't indigestion after all," he said softly.

"What?"

"Look. There's an opening up here. Kind of jagged and narrow, but maybe big enough for a smallish person if you're careful. Dry too, and looks like it might expand to a bigger space once you're through."

Her gaze followed his and she jumped up and

down, trying to see inside. She knew it was probably nothing but couldn't help feeling a ping of excitement anyway.

"I'll give you a boost." He put down his lantern and threaded his fingers together, palms up. "Step in my hands."

"Let me take my boot off first. Or better yet, I'll get on your shoulders and climb in so you don't have to lift my full weight."

"What, you think I'm a wimpy weakling?" He stopped her as she reached for her boot. "I'm wearing gloves, and you might get your sock all wet."

Wimpy weakling? She shook her head and grinned at the man who was about as far from that description as a human could possibly be. "Fine. But don't complain if you throw out your back."

She stepped into his palms and he lifted her so high, she was able to grab onto the edges and peer inside, the glow of her headlamp lighting the space. "It's big inside here, but kind of strange. Different from the cave we just came through."

"How do you mean?"

"There are chunks of stone and broken stalactites everywhere. And like you said, the crevice is real jagged instead of smooth like the cave walls."

"Aeons of moisture and minerals have glazed these walls. Since this crevice isn't like that, there's a reason. Like maybe the earthquake a few weeks ago opened it when it had never been open before."

She looked down at him, his eyes vibrant and alive as they met hers. "Maybe you're right."

"Come back down. We'll grab the tools and open it up wider so we can both get inside."

Andros found a few sizable rocks to roll over beneath the crevice that they could stand on as they whacked at the edges of the opening. "Turn your head when you swing, so you don't end up with shards in your eyes. I hate removing stuff from people's corneas."

"And I'd hate it to be my cornea you had to remove stuff from." Looking at him balancing on that rock, a smile in his eyes as they stood close together in this corner working away, made her insides feel all gooey.

"Thanks for helping me. I really appreciate it."

"Like you left me a choice. I would've been a nervous wreck thinking of you getting lost in this cave. Not to mention I didn't want to have to spend my whole day off tomorrow hunting for you when you didn't show up for dinner."

"You don't fool me. I think you're enjoying this. It's an adventure, right?" She turned her head and closed her eyes as she gave another mighty swing at the crevice edge. Though mighty was probably an overstatement, since Andros had already bashed out a good six inches from top to bottom on his side.

"Okay, I admit it. It's intriguing." He leaned back and surveyed their work. "I think it's big enough. Come on, I'll help you up, then follow you in."

She stuck her foot in his hands again, and when she was halfway in he let go and cupped her derriere in his hands, shoving her far enough in that she was able to squirm the rest of the way and stand up. "Was that an excuse to fondle me?"

"Do I need an excuse?" He boosted himself in to stand in front of her, sliding his hand around her rear again and pulling her close.

She chuckled. "I guess not." She gave him another one of those paper-mask kisses, their eyes meeting over the top. "You realize I'm sorely tempted to pull down this stupid thing and kiss you for real."

"Me too. But we'll save that for a little later, hmm?" He grasped her hand as they picked their way over all the broken rock littering the ground. "This place definitely had a huge seismic shift just recently for there to be so much of this. I—holy Apollo, Laurel."

"What? What?" She looked all around, trying to aim her headlamp where he was looking.

"Something's back here, behind this tall half-broken wall. Gleaming, like metal."

Laurel didn't realize she'd stopped breathing, her heart pounding so hard it echoed in her head, until they stepped around the wall and every bit of air left her lungs in a gasp. "Oh, Andros."

Together, they stared silently at the stunning, life-sized gold statue of Artemis, gleaming as brightly as if it had just been polished by an ancient hand. She stood beautifully perfect beneath an arching ceiling, coins and jewels scattered around her feet in what had probably been homage to Apollo's sister.

Tears stung Laurel's eyes and throat, and a small sob burst from her mouth, muffled by the mask.

She turned to Andros, and saw the same awe and amazement on his eyes she knew was in her own.

"You did it, Laurel. You didn't stop believing, didn't stop trying. This is…incredible."

"I'm not sure I didn't stop believing, but I wanted to believe, so much." She reached to touch it, reverently sliding her hand over the statue's intricately detailed gown, her ethereal face.

"Your parents would be so proud."

"They would. Yes, they would. Oh, my God, I can hardly soak it in."

She flung her arms around his neck and buried her face in his shoulder, letting the tears flow as his arms came around her. Tears of happiness and relief and joy, knowing her parents' work would be highlighted once more. Thinking how proud they'd be that she—with Andros's help—had actually found this spectacular treasure.

"Thank you, Andros," she whispered. "Thank you for helping me. For seeing the crevice. Hammering it open. For spotting…her. I…I don't think we'd be standing here in front of her if you hadn't."

His hands slowly stroked up and down her back. "Oh, you would have found her. That stubborn streak of yours would have kicked in, and who knows? Maybe that feeling Tom had would have come to guide you too."

She looked up, blinking at her tears. "I think maybe there's a part of you that believed in that feeling. That kind of guidance."

"Maybe." His eyes crinkled at the corners. "So now what, Ms. Evans? Who do you need to contact?"

"First, I—*Aahh!*"

They both ducked, startled by something swooping by their ears. Andros straightened and looked around, his brows lowered in a thoughtful frown. "I asked Tom if he'd seen bats in the cave, and he said no. But that was definitely a bat."

He released her and walked around, looking carefully at the various corners of the cave where he pointed his headlamp. "Bat guano. A lot of it." He looked upward, aiming the light around the ceiling that was much higher in this cave than the other one. "Bingo! Hundreds of bats curled up there sleeping. See them?"

"Okay, now I know for sure why I preferred working on the mountain instead of in here." She shuddered, creeped out by the creatures hanging shoulder to shoulder, as far along the cave ceiling as they could see. "Glad we found Artemis pretty fast."

"Bat guano, Laurel." He stared at her, a new excitement in his voice and gleaming in his eyes. "It can be a primary source of coronavirus infection if it's breathed into the lungs."

"Coronavirus? You mean like SARS and MERS?"

"Probably a mutated strain. Pneumonia is the most common clinical presentation of coronavirus, sometimes with nausea and diarrhea like Jason had. Renal failure and pericarditis. Sepsis, which we couldn't manage well for John. It all makes sense now!"

He grabbed her shoulders, practically dancing her around. "The reason no one got sick before the past couple weeks was because the bats were in this cave, not the one your crew was working in. Then the recent earthquake opened up that crevice, and the bats flew into the dig cave. Tom and Jason worked all day, breathing in the airborne dissemination of the virus."

"But what about Becka? She worked in the cave

all day and didn't get sick. And Mel wasn't in here at all."

"Some people carry the virus, but never show symptoms, which could be the situation with Becka. And while coronavirus is primarily contracted through respiratory exposure to guano or animal secretions, like from camels carrying MERS, it can be contracted from very close person-to-person contact."

"So you've solved the mystery." Her excitement began to match his and she laughed as they did another little two-step around the cave. "Nobody in Kastorini or Delphi has to worry they'll get it. You're a genius!"

"We solved it together." He cupped the back of her head with his hand. "I never would have come in here if you hadn't."

"And Artemis might have stayed hidden forever." They looked at one another, and Laurel's heart swelled and squeezed at the same time. "Do you think she was hidden by the earthquake my parents died in? That maybe the only entrance got shut down to anything bigger than a bat?"

"More likely an earthquake from a thousand years ago, and if that's the case your parents would never have found it." He tipped his forehead against hers, speaking softly. "Maybe the gods felt bad about that, about the tragedy, and made another earthquake happen just for you in their memory."

"Yes. In their memory." She gave him a fierce hug, unable to identify all the powerful emotions swirling around inside her. They were grief and joy, sadness and amazement, and Andros was somehow wrapped up in every one of them.

"We have some work in front of us, Ms. Evans," he said, his voice that low rumble in her ear that always made her quiver inside. "I need to talk to Di and get the national infection control folks out here, take some samples. Have them check the blood work we have from your team to confirm it. And once it is, contact the media to calm the fears they stirred up before."

"And I have to call Tom and Mel and tell them we did it. They'll talk to the university while I contact the Greek Archaeological Society." She squeezed him tighter. "I can't wait to tell my sisters too."

"We should probably call the authorities to protect the statue. I doubt anyone would come in here, and it's hidden well, but, since it appears to be solid gold, I'm thinking there are one or two people who would like to get their hands on it."

"Except she probably weighs a zillion pounds."

"There's that." He chuckled. "I'll call Georgo, the police chief in Kastorini, and let him handle it however he thinks. He's an old friend and as honest as they come."

She slowly pulled herself from his arms. Holding his hand, she carefully stroked the statue one more time. "Thanks for showing yourself to us, beautiful. I know whoever created you as a gift to Apollo loved you, but it's time for the rest of the world to love you even more."

Andros gripped her hand and when she turned to him she was surprised to see his eyes were now deeply serious. "And I have a feeling the world will love her finder as well."

The rosy-gold sky was darkening around the mountains, the waters of the gulf a deeper blue from the low light, when Laurel and Andros finished what seemed like a never-ending number of calls and emails.

"Okay," Andros said, "I think we can finally relax and celebrate."

Laurel glanced up from her laptop, her heart skipping a beat as she looked at the man leaning against the kitchen doorjamb. He'd showered and changed, and his slightly damp black hair was curling a bit around his ears and at the nape of his neck. His snug jeans rode a little low on his hips, and a white polo shirt was startlingly bright against his bronzed skin.

She let herself soak in the sight of him, that uncomfortable swirl of emotions back in spades.

There was no denying she was crazy about this man. Smart, caring, and beyond beautiful inside and out. She adored his little girl and felt warmed and welcomed by this lovely town they lived in. Liked his sister too, and had a feeling she'd like his parents just as well.

But she would never know, because she had to leave. With Andros's help, she'd accomplished her goal, big time. Now could finish her PhD dissertation. Get the grant paperwork done and in, making sure the wheels were greased to get her dig in Turkey going when she got the grant money, which shouldn't be a question now. She'd assemble a team. Lots of qualified applicants would want to be a part of it after this monumental discovery. And there would be interviews galore— while she talked about her parents' conviction that they'd find the statue there, she'd take that opportunity to talk about her own upcoming dig, knowing her parents would feel satisfied and happy that she'd accomplished the dream they'd had for her.

All that should leave her feeling elated. But battling with that elation was the heavy reality that she'd be saying goodbye to this place. To Andros. She couldn't deny she wasn't ready to do that. Wasn't sure she'd ever be ready.

She managed a smile, determined to enjoy her last day or two with him. "We've earned a celebration for sure. What did you have in mind?"

His eyes took on a wicked glint, and his slow smile sent her heart rate zooming. How could a single look from a man make her feel like throwing him to the floor to have her way with him?

"Let's start with an aperitif. I got white wine for you, but of course I have retsina and ouzo as well."

"You know, believe it or not I do have a taste for retsina tonight. And maybe a little of that grilled octopus you say the restaurant down the street does so well."

"Yeah?" He took a few steps closer, and she set her laptop aside so she could stand and meet him halfway. "Sounds like you've become part Greek. Part of Kastorini."

"Maybe I have." Her eyes drifted closed as he pressed soft kisses on her temple, her cheek, the corner of her mouth. Her words echoed in her head, making her chest ache. *Maybe I have. Or maybe this place has become a part of me.*

"So, about you becoming part of Kastorini." The pads of his fingers slowly slipped across all the places he'd just kissed, ending up warmly cupping the side of her throat. His expression was surprisingly serious, at odds with his teasing voice. "You already know Greece is the epicenter of history just waiting for an archaeologist to find and share it?"

"Spoken like a true Greek, especially one born near the belly button of the entire earth," she said. "But a lot of other countries might argue with that perspective, Dr. Drakoulias. Not only in Europe, but China and South America and—"

He pressed his mouth to hers, effectively shutting her up. When he broke the kiss, his lips were curved, but his eyes still held that peculiar seriousness. Though she shouldn't think it was odd, since she found herself feeling very serious too.

"I know your passion is Greek archaeology," he said. She looked at him and nodded, though front and foremost in her mind at that moment was an entirely differently passion of hers. Passion for the man standing right in front of her. The man who stole her breath and had managed to steal a scarily large chunk of her heart as well. "But at the moment, there's a different subject on my mind."

"I might be able to guess what it is," she managed to say in a teasingly light voice.

"Probably not." His hands tightened on her. "I just wanted to say I wish we'd met in a different place in our lives. Before you had your exciting dig plans stretching out in front of you, and before I had Cassie to think about, raising her here in Kastorini. But we didn't."

"No," she whispered. "We didn't."

"I'd ask you to come back and visit sometime when you're in Greece again, but I know that's not the best idea. Cassie already likes you a lot, and since she lost her mother I don't want her to become attached to someone who's not going to be around long. And, I...well, you know I'm not a guy with a very good track record. But I want you to know that I'll really miss you."

"I'll miss you too." As she spoke she thought about what he'd said. And was filled with the bizarre thought that someday, when she worked in Greece again, she could visit Andros and see if, maybe, they might both be in a different place then. That Cassie might need another mother figure. And if they were, who knew? Maybe—

The door burst open, and they both swiveled toward it to see Taryn run in, frazzled and breathless. Andros let go of Laurel and strode to his sister. "What's wrong?"

"Have you seen the kids? They were playing in the backyard, but when I went to get them for dinner they were gone. I looked around but don't see them anywhere. And it's almost dark." She sucked in a breath. "They must be here, right?"

CHAPTER FOURTEEN

LAUREL FOUGHT DOWN her rising fear as the three of
them searched for Cassie and Petros. It was nearly
impossible for Laurel to keep up with Andros as he
strode down streets and narrow alleyways, shining his flashlight into garden plots and patches of
forest, calling the children's names in a voice loud
enough to carry a long way through the inky night.
Kastorini might be fairly small, but in the dark one
house looked pretty much like another, so she tried
to stick as close to him as she could. Last thing he
needed was to worry about her being lost too.

"Let's check the schoolyard," Andros said in a
controlled but obviously tense voice. "They both
like to play there."

"But they've never tried to go alone, even during the day," Taryn said, sounding breathless and
near tears. "I can't believe they'd go that far at
night."

The terror in Taryn's voice clutched at Lauren's

heart and brought back the frightening memory of her sister being missing, just a few months after her mom and dad had died. Helen had ridden her bike to a friend's house and hadn't come home for dinner. Laurel still remembered the icy panic she'd felt when she'd called and found Helen had left the friend's nearly an hour earlier.

She'd jumped into her car and driven up and down the streets Helen would have ridden on, but she wasn't anywhere to be seen. Her chest had filled with an unbearable fear as questions swirled in her head. Had Helen been abducted? Had she done something crazy in her grief over their parents? How could she have gotten lost? Laurel remembered nearly weeping in relief when it had turned out her sweet baby sister had just gotten a flat tire on her bike and decided to take a short-cut when she walked it home.

It had been the first moment, one of many to come, that Laurel had doubted she was capable of taking on the care and guidance of her sisters full-time.

"We've looked close to home," Andros said. "We need to think of where they like to go, what they might be thinking."

A number of neighbors had joined the hunt, spreading out through the town. "Cassie was excited telling me about fishing with you and Laurel," Taryn said. "Surely they wouldn't go to the boat."

Andros swung around to look at his sister, a low curse on his breath. "Neither of them can really swim. Come on."

They switched direction. Laurel thought they were heading to the stone steps down to the water and could hear the rising anxiety in both their voices. Could feel it in her own heart. An olive branch snagged her hair, and she had to stop to pull it loose. Then stared at the tree, an overwhelming conviction smacking straight between her eyes.

"The fairies!" she called out to Andros and Taryn as she hurried to catch up. "You know Cassie and Petros have been obsessed with fairies and monsters. Remember when I told her they liked olive wood, and she asked if I thought they lived in the olive groves? They both asked me about it again and if monsters might live there too."

Andros stopped and stared at her, his eyes glittering through the blackness of the night. He yanked out his phone and dialed. "Georgo, check to see if they might have gone to my boat on the water. We're going to the east olive groves." He hung up the call. "This way, Laurel." He grabbed her hand, and they backtracked up the steps and onto a dirt path. "You just might be right, and I hope to God you are."

After a five-minute near run to the grove, and another twenty minutes searching and calling, Laurel began to despair. She nearly blurted out the question she kept wondering, which was how long would it take to find them in the midst of thousands of trees? And how much time were they wasting if the kids weren't here?

But she managed to bite her lip, nearly drawing blood. Last thing Andros and Taryn needed was for her to pile on more doubt and fear with a stupid and obvious comment.

Andros came to such an abrupt stop, she nearly bumped into his back.

"What?" Taryn asked with wide eyes. "Do you—?"

He held up his hand. "Shh. I thought I heard them answer." He cupped his hands around his mouth, bellowing out to them, and Laurel's heart nearly stopped when she heard what might have been an answering cry.

"Petros!" Taryn nearly screamed her son's name and took off running through the trees, Andros moving in the same direction but veering more to the left. Laurel realized it made sense to spread out some and went in the other direction, trying to search for the kids with the flashlight, somehow watching where she was going at the same time.

Her entire heart felt lodged inside her throat as she called to them. Her ears strained to hear something, anything, and suddenly the small voices were in front of her. "Cassie! Petros!"

"Laurel!" The little girl sounded terrified.

"Oh, my God, Cassie, where are you?" She swung the flashlight through the trees, the light picking up eerie shadows she kept thinking were the children, and suddenly they were there. They rushed into the beam of light, both children grabbing her legs and crying.

"I thought I heard my mommy," Petros sobbed. "I thought I heard her and Uncle Andros."

"They're here. They're both here. You're fine. You're safe." She crouched down and hugged them against her, tears clogging her throat. She swallowed them down so she could let Andros and Taryn know she had them.

"Here! Over here!"

A dark shaped loomed out of the darkness. Andros. He swung both children into his arms, kissing their cheeks, then pressed his face against Cassie's hair. "You both scared us to death. Don't ever, ever leave the house without telling us. You hear me?"

Both nodded, and Cassie snaked her arms around his neck in what looked like a stranglehold. "I'm sorry, Daddy. Laurel told us there were fairies in the olive trees. But then it got dark and we didn't know how to get home."

The little sob in her voice stabbed straight into Laurel's heart and she took a step back, her hands clutching at her chest as Taryn ran up to hold Petros.

This was all her fault. Why hadn't she realized she shouldn't say something like that to a small child? She'd always known she hadn't truly been up to the task of raising her sisters. So how could she have just been thinking there might be a time she'd like to come back to Kastorini? To see if this something between her and Andros could blossom into something more? To mother this beautiful child?

"I have to leave," she said as she turned away, her heart feeling shredded from the anxiety of the past hour. From guilt and misery at her own inadequacy. She wasn't sure if she'd said it to herself or Andros or the fairies in the olive grove, but she now knew without a doubt she had to go.

Laurel rested her hand on the windowsill in Andros's living room, staring out at the night. Wishing she could see the charming homes with their terracotta roofs and tumble of vibrant flowers, the crooked little streets, the cats sitting grooming themselves by doors so colorful and intriguing they could have been from a story, making her want to walk through and read the next chapter.

But it was probably just as well the darkness shrouded it all. She'd be leaving in the morning, and the look and feel of this town was etched forever in her mind and heart anyway.

She heard the stairs creak but didn't turn. Sensed rather than heard Andros coming to stand behind her. His hands resting on her shoulders were warm and heavy. Adding to the weight she already felt there.

"She's sound asleep. I guess an adventure and scare like that takes it out of a little girl."

And big ones, too. "I'm willing to bet she and Petros stick close to home from now on." She turned, swallowing down the tears that formed in her throat again. "I'm so sorry I thoughtlessly talked about the fairies living in the olive groves. This was all my fault."

"Don't be ridiculous." His hands tightened on her shoulders. "You couldn't have known they'd get it in their heads to go there."

"I have three sisters. I watched them a lot when they were little. And after I took on their care full-time, I learned the hard way to be careful what I said. To think before I spoke when they talked about boyfriend crises and school dramas and plans to move to the Amazon jungle alone to study indigenous peoples."

"Laurel. Every parent does or says things they later wish they hadn't."

"I'm not a parent. Not anymore. And I can't be. I just finished that role, and I wasn't very good at it. I...I have a plan for my life, and I need to get started on that plan." A plan that, just hours earlier, she hadn't been 100 percent certain she wanted so very much anymore.

His gaze seemed to search her face for a long time before he finally nodded, tugging her closer to press the gentlest of kisses on each of her cheeks before fully pulling her into his arms and simply holding her. She wrapped her arms around his back and breathed him in, wanting to imprint his scent and the feel of his body on hers one last time.

She tilted her head up to look at him, touching his face, wanting to also imprint every beautiful feature of his face in her memories. Though she didn't really need to do that, as she'd committed it to memory weeks ago. It seemed perhaps he was doing the same, as he looked at her for long moments before he lowered his mouth to hers and kissed her.

Soft and sweet, the kiss was also filled with a melancholy, then with a growing heat until Andros pulled back and set her away from him. His chest lifted with a deep breath before he spoke.

"You need me to do anything for you before you leave?"

There was only one thing that came to mind. "Yes." She stepped close again and wrapped her arms around his neck, but he grasped her forearms before she could kiss him.

"Laurel. We shouldn't. You mean more to me than a night of sex before you're out of my life forever. That's not who I am anymore, and it will just make saying goodbye even harder."

"Maybe it will. But you mean more to me too." She stroked his cheek, cupped it in her hand. "I don't think it would be wrong for two people who care about one another to make love before they say goodbye, do you?"

"Maybe it wouldn't." He pressed his lips to her palm, lingered there. "Maybe the truth is I'm just trying to keep my heart intact here. But one thing I do know is that being with you one more time would be worth a few more bruises tomorrow."

The small smile he gave her added to the pain and pleasure swirling around her heart. "I agree." She tugged his head down to her and kissed him. Long and slow and with a building passion that weakened her knees.

He drew back. "Cassie almost never gets out of bed, but in case she has a nightmare or something we should go to my room. Come on."

He grasped her hand and led her to his bedroom. A comfortable-looking masculine space she'd peeked into but hadn't been inside. He shut and locked the door behind them. Holding her gaze, he gently tugged her hair loose from her ponytail. His fingers slowly stroked down the length of it, then he touched her forehead, her cheekbones, and chin with his fingertips as well. Much the same way she'd touched the Artemis statue, with a reverence on his face that made her ache. He finally reached for the buttons of her blouse, and with each one he flicked open, her breath grew shallower, her anticipation ratcheted higher.

"You are so beautiful, Laurel." He slipped the blouse from her shoulders, ran his fingertips across the lace of her bra until she shivered.

"As are you." She tunneled her hands beneath his shirt, loving the way his muscles tightened at her touch. Stroked her palms through the soft hair on his chest until impatience got the better of her and, with his help, she yanked it over his head and off. She wrapped her arms around him, pressed her lips to his warmth, and he seemed suddenly impatient as well, flicking off her bra and quickly undoing her pants, shoving them down and off, along with her panties, in one swift movement.

She wasn't sure how he managed to kiss her breathless, shuck his own pants and settle them onto the bed in a matter of moments, but it didn't matter. His lips caressed her throat, her collarbone, her breasts. His fingers moved over her skin and teased her everywhere, and she closed her eyes to soak in the delicious sensations one last time. And when the pressure built until it was nearly unbearable, he finally joined her. Twined his fingers with hers, palms pressed together, eyes meeting in a deep connection that went far beyond the physical one they were sharing.

"Laurel. Laurel." He whispered her name as he took her further, higher, and his name was on her lips when they fell.

CHAPTER FIFTEEN

LAUREL SAT IN the university's office for the archaeology school and stared at the letter in her hand, waiting to feel the jubilation that should have her jumping up and down. The letter announcing that her grant application had been approved, and the dig she'd planned in Turkey could begin as soon as she had the equipment scheduled, accommodations booked and a crew pulled together.

Her gaze slid to the sturdy cardboard envelope lying on her desk that held her doctorate diploma, and while she was proud of it, she didn't feel the elation she knew she should feel by having completed both those accomplishments in the past month.

And she knew why. Making love with Andros had felt so bittersweet, leaving her with even more memories of him that now filled her with more sadness than pleasure. He'd been right when he'd said it would just make it harder to say goodbye. *Had* made saying goodbye harder, or would have if she'd stayed long enough to say it.

Hours of tender kisses and lying quietly together, arms and legs entwined, had left her with too many emotions tangled up as well. And when she'd finally slipped away to the guest room so Cassie wouldn't wake up to them in bed together, she'd been unable to sleep. Thinking of leaving in a few hours, and saying goodbye to Kastorini. To everyone she'd become fond of. To Andros and Cassie, whom she'd become far more than fond of.

So she'd left, slipping out of the door and driving to the airport before dawn. Leaving a note had seemed like the best kind of closure, but now she realized it had been cowardly. She'd wanted to avoid the pain of those farewells, but the only thing that had accomplished was to leave her with a deep ache. Without a sense of closure after all.

She sighed and tried to pull her attention back to work. While she concentrated on making a long to-do list for the project in Turkey, Mel came into the office and leaned down to give her a hug.

"I heard about your grant, girl. Congratulations,

you deserve it! Your parents would be so incredibly proud of all you've accomplished."

"I know. They would." And she was glad. Glad to know they'd be proud, in comparison to all the times they hadn't been so proud. All the times she hadn't quite lived up to the standards they'd set for her.

"And yet you don't seem very happy." Mel sat in the chair next to the desk and rested her elbow on it. "What's going on?"

"Nothing. I'm happy. Just tired, I guess. My moment of fame, being interviewed for magazines and on TV, has been pretty exhausting, I've got to say." She kept her voice light and joking, but knew Mel would probably see right through it.

"Mmm-hmm. More so than working ten solid hours digging rocks on a hot mountainside, which never seemed to exhaust you. So tell me the truth."

Laurel leaned back in the swivel chair, and just the thought of telling Mel made her feel like a traitor to her parents. To their dreams. "I achieved everything I wanted to this year. Got my doctorate, the grant money, and most incredibly, we found the statue. There's clearly something wrong with me that it doesn't feel like…enough."

"Maybe because it's not what you really wanted after all."

"Of course it is. I wanted to finish this dig for Mom and Dad, and I wanted to get going on the achievements they planned for me."

"What do you want for yourself?"

Laurel stared at her. "I already told you. Their work—"

"Exactly. *Their* work. Which doesn't have to be yours, Laurel. I know, as their oldest, they always expected—demanded—a lot of you. You took on the care of your sisters, which wasn't easy. Took on your grad studies, then took on the task of finishing the Delphi dig, with spectacular success. So why do you feel like that's not enough?"

She stared at Mel, gathering her thoughts. Asking herself that question. "Because it's not. For years, they talked about me heading up a dig as soon as I got my PhD. Planned to help make it happen so I'd get started in that role even younger than they were. I may be behind, but I still want to make it happen."

"For you, or for them, to fulfill their dream for you? Maybe it's time for you to ask yourself if what you thought you wanted is really just what *they* wanted." Mel reached to hold her hand. "Maybe focusing on all this has been your way of unconsciously dealing with the grief that's still inside you over your parents dying. A way to come to peace with that."

Stunned, Laurel met Mel's gaze. Was it possible she'd convinced herself she wanted to do the project in Turkey for that reason? Not because that was what called to her professionally?

"I…I don't know. But I do love archaeology. I love digging and finding and recording history. Really, I do."

"I know you do. Just think about the rest of it, will you?" Mel squeezed her hand. "By the way, Helen called me. Said she'd been trying to get hold of you and wanted me to tell you."

"Okay, thanks."

She stared at Mel as she left the room, still confused by their conversation, then dialed her sister. "Hey, sweetie, what's up?"

"Hi, Laurel! Guess what?"

She smiled at the enthusiasm in her bubbly little sister's voice. "What?"

"Professor Green said he wants me to come back to this dig next summer, after I'm finished with my first year of college! Do you really think it'll be a good thing to put on my grad-school applications?"

"Congrats! Yes, it definitely will. I'm proud of you for working hard and going for it." As soon as the words came out of her mouth, she wondered if she sounded exactly like her parents. Pushing instead of just encouraging. "But you may find other things you want to study after this coming year. Don't feel like you have to plan your whole future right this minute."

"Okay, I won't. Thanks for being the best big sister ever and for always giving me good advice."

Her heart squished at her sister's words. "I don't think I've always done that so well."

"Sure you have. I want to tell you how much I love you for that. How much all three of us do."

"I love you too." Laurel stared at the phone after they said their goodbyes. Realizing that all her sisters had said sweet things like this before, but she hadn't really heard them. Had she been too worried about how she was "failing" at being a parent to notice the things she might be doing right?

Maybe she'd been mistaken about a lot of things she'd been so sure of. And if she had been, maybe it was time to get it right.

"There's another picture of Laurel, Daddy!"

Cassie's stubby finger pointed at the photo in the magazine, but she hadn't needed to. Most readers probably focused on the pictures of the spectacular golden statue he'd been blessed enough to help find, but he saw only Laurel. Her intelligent blue eyes, her sweet, smiling lips, her beautiful face. Her hair—hair that he knew all too well felt silky soft within his fingers—spilling in golden waves over her shoulders.

"Yes. There are quite a few pictures of her in these magazines, aren't there?"

"Why?"

"Because the statue was an amazing find. There's nothing like it in the whole world, and Laurel's the one who kept looking for it."

"You helped her. You found it too. Why isn't your picture in here with hers?"

He wished there were photos of the two of them together, but it wasn't meant to be. Probably his penance for the years he'd dismissed the idea of a real relationship with a woman. Known he didn't have it in him.

But the way he'd missed Laurel the past month had him wondering if maybe he was capable of it, after all. That maybe he'd just needed to meet the right woman to feel that kind of commitment. Except she was traveling the world, and he had Cassie to raise here.

"She's the archaeologist. I just got lucky to be with her that day." And a few other magical days. More than lucky.

"Thea Taryn showed me your picture in the other magazine. The one about people getting sick. Laurel helped you figure that out, didn't she?"

"Yes. We made a good team." And as he said the words, the hollowness he'd felt since the moment he'd woken up and found her gone seemed to widen a little more.

"Why aren't you still, Daddy? A team with Laurel?"

He looked down into her wide eyes and his lips twisted a little, thinking what a simple question it was. One with a simple answer. "Her work takes her on adventures all over the world, Cassie. Our home is here in Kastorini, with Yiayia and Papou and Thea Taryn and Petros and everyone else."

"I like adventures, Daddy. And doctors can help people anywhere. Why can't we go on adventures with Laurel and come home to visit everybody sometimes?"

Her words were so matter-of-fact, the expression in her eyes telling him she thought he might be a little dense. And as he stared at her he wondered the same damn thing.

He'd brought Cassie to Kastorini because he'd thought that was where the newly mature doctor with a daughter needed to be. Taken his place beside his father, even though the man had practiced medicine for years without any problems finding a temporary replacement when he'd needed to.

He'd disliked being judged by the town, worried about disappointing his parents, couldn't let Cassie be exposed to gossip or become attached to a woman he might selfishly date for just a short time. But didn't part of growing into a responsible adult bring with it a responsibility to himself too?

"You may be onto something there, *koukla mou*. Maybe an adventure with Laurel is exactly what we need."

* * *

Laurel's hands were sweating on the steering wheel of her rental car as she drove up Mount Parnassus and parked. She got out and stared at the mountain, which hadn't changed since she'd left a month ago. Hadn't changed in aeons. Then turned to look at the incredible blue waters of the gulf that stretched to mountains on the other side and to the sea of olive trees flowing down to meet it.

She'd loved this place the moment she'd arrived. Loved it even more after living in Kastorini for a few days.

Loved the man who'd been born here and was a part of this place, and she hoped and prayed he wanted her to be a part of it too.

He'd been silent for a moment when she'd called to tell him she'd come back to Delphi on business. Didn't tell him it was personal business, because it was too important to talk about on the phone. Too critical to her future happiness.

She walked up the goat path, stopping a few times to lift her face to the brilliant sun. To the intense heat she loved. When she finally got to the closed dig site, she moved slowly to the pit that had collapsed during the earthquake five years ago. The pit where her parents had died.

She knelt, picturing the horrific scene as she had so many times before. But this time felt different. Their spirits were there with her on the mountain, and they were smiling at her, holding her, encouraging her. Not judging her, not disappointed in her. The occasional strife of their relationship that had lodged itself too long in her brain faded away, leaving only the good memories of all their years together.

"I love you, Mom. Dad. Thank you for everything you gave me, including my love of archaeology. And most especially my sisters."

She kissed her fingers and pressed them to the ground for a moment. Then stood, and, when she turned, saw a beautiful Greek man walking surefooted and steady up the goat path, looking exactly as he had the first time she'd seen him. She smiled and her heart swelled at the same time that nervous jitters quivered in her stomach.

She made her way back down the steep path to meet him. "Hi." It wasn't a very original greeting, but all her rehearsed words seemed to evaporate when she looked into the dark eyes she'd missed so much.

"Hi." His lips curved just a little and he took another step closer, until they nearly touched. "You called me to help you find another statue up here?"

"No. I…I hope you'll help me find something else."

"What's that?"

"I lost my happy after I left here. I'm hoping you can help me find it again."

His dark eyes stared into hers as his hands cupped her waist. "I'll do whatever I can to help you. But here's something funny. I need your help with the same damn thing."

In a sudden movement, he tugged her flat against him and kissed her. She clung to him, the heat of his mouth and the sun burning down on them making her dizzy.

"I almost fell over when the phone rang and it was you," he said, "because I'd just pulled it from my pocket to call you. Must have been that sixth sense you and Tom believe in."

"Why were you going to call?"

"Because I realized I hadn't followed the wisdom of the stone at Delphi that says 'Know thyself.' That I believed I had, but was focused instead on who I thought I was, who I thought I needed to be. Not on who I could be."

"Me too," she whispered. "I—"

"I need you to know why I'd decided to call." He pressed his fingers to her lips. "I wanted to tell the incredible woman I'm crazy in love with that a four-year-old girl is smarter than I am. That we don't have to stay put in Kastorini. We can travel to be wherever you are, so you can do the work you love. I don't care where we live and neither does she. I just want to be with you, if you'll let me."

"Oh, Andros." She sniffed back stupid tears. "I came to tell you I love Kastorini. I love Cassie, and most of all I love you. So much. I realized I wanted to be in Kastorini with you and Cassie, which could work if I concentrate on digs in Greece instead of other places. And I realized that working around the world wouldn't make me happy if you weren't with me."

He lifted one hand to cup her cheek, tunneling his fingers into her hair. "Cassie told me we make a good team. Maybe that means we do both. We live in Kastorini when you don't have to be on a dig outside Greece, and we live wherever your work takes you when you do."

"That would…be good. Perfect, even." She reached up to kiss him but he pulled back.

"There's one more important thing I need to ask." He grasped her hands, and went down on one knee in the dirt, wincing when his knee rolled onto a stone.

"Come back up." She tried to tug him, but it was like lifting the statue of Artemis. Or Apollo. "You don't need to do this."

"I want to do this." His eyes met hers. "Laurel Evans, I love you more than I knew it was possible to love a woman. Will you marry me? Be my wife? My forever teammate, wherever it takes us?"

The emotion in his voice had her choking back tears again. "Yes. I will. And, darn it, come up here so I can kiss you."

"One more minute." He reached into his pocket. "It's not a ring, yet, but maybe it will do until I can get one. Hold out your wrist."

She looked down and gasped when she saw a

bracelet circled with gleaming moonstones. "How did you find time to run to the store to get this?" she asked as she held out her hand.

"I bought it after you left." His gaze was suddenly serious as he looked up from fastening it to her wrist. "I thought maybe if I held it close in my hand, it would keep you safe on your travels. Maybe even be that love talisman you talked about. Bring you back to me someday."

"Oh, Andros," she whispered, swallowing hard at another lump in her throat. "What did I say before about the charm of Greek men? How can I possibly resist the power of a moonstone? And of you."

"I hope you can't." He grinned as he rose, and that elusive dimple poked into his cheek. She laughed and sniffled and kissed it first, before she pressed her mouth to his to seal the deal. "Thank you," he whispered against her lips. "I promise to do everything I can to make you happy."

"Being a team of three will definitely make me happy. With maybe a few more recruits when we're ready."

As he kissed her again, the warmth of him wrapped her with joy, and she didn't think it was her imagination that she just might be hearing the music of god Apollo from the mountaintop, playing in celebration.

* * * * *

MILLS & BOON®
Large Print Medical

January

Unlocking Her Surgeon's Heart	Fiona Lowe
Her Playboy's Secret	Tina Beckett
The Doctor She Left Behind	Scarlet Wilson
Taming Her Navy Doc	Amy Ruttan
A Promise...to a Proposal?	Kate Hardy
Her Family for Keeps	Molly Evans

February

Hot Doc from Her Past	Tina Beckett
Surgeons, Rivals...Lovers	Amalie Berlin
Best Friend to Perfect Bride	Jennifer Taylor
Resisting Her Rebel Doc	Joanna Neil
A Baby to Bind Them	Susanne Hampton
Doctor...to Duchess?	Annie O'Neil

March

Falling at the Surgeon's Feet	Lucy Ryder
One Night in New York	Amy Ruttan
Daredevil, Doctor...Husband?	Alison Roberts
The Doctor She'd Never Forget	Annie Claydon
Reunited...in Paris!	Sue MacKay
French Fling to Forever	Karin Baine

MILLS & BOON®
Large Print Medical

April

The Baby of Their Dreams — Carol Marinelli
Falling for Her Reluctant Sheikh — Amalie Berlin
Hot-Shot Doc, Secret Dad — Lynne Marshall
Father for Her Newborn Baby — Lynne Marshall
His Little Christmas Miracle — Emily Forbes
Safe in the Surgeon's Arms — Molly Evans

May

A Touch of Christmas Magic — Scarlet Wilson
Her Christmas Baby Bump — Robin Gianna
Winter Wedding in Vegas — Janice Lynn
One Night Before Christmas — Susan Carlisle
A December to Remember — Sue MacKay
A Father This Christmas? — Louisa Heaton

June

Playboy Doc's Mistletoe Kiss — Tina Beckett
Her Doctor's Christmas Proposal — Louisa George
From Christmas to Forever? — Marion Lennox
A Mummy to Make Christmas — Susanne Hampton
Miracle Under the Mistletoe — Jennifer Taylor
His Christmas Bride-to-Be — Abigail Gordon